Land of burning heat

Land of Burning Heat

a Claire Reynier mystery

JUDITH van GIESON

University of New Mexico Press
Albuquerque

Land of Burning Heat

© Judith Van Gieson, 2003

Published by the University of New Mexico Press by
arrangement with Signet, a division of Penguin Putnam, Inc.

First edition

Library of Congress Cataloging-in-Publication Data

Van Gieson, Judith

Land of burning heat : a Claire Reynier mystery /
Judith Van Gieson.—1st ed.

p. cm.

ISBN 0-8263-3172-6 (cloth : alk. paper)

1. Reynier, Claire (Fictitious character)—Fiction. 2. Jews—
Persecutions—Fiction. 3. Women archivists—Fiction.
4. Jews—Mexico—Fiction. 5. Manuscripts—Fiction.
6. New Mexico—Fiction. I. Title.

PS3572.A42224 L36 2003

813'.54—dc21   2002152988

Publisher's Note

For my stepfather,
Richard Zieger

Many thanks to Irene Marcuse, Lou Hieb, Julie Mars, Ann Paden, Mike Clover, and Maria Senaida Velasquez Huerta. I am blessed to have such knowledgeable friends who were willing to read the manuscript of *Land of Burning Heat* and share their expertise in many areas including Judaism, academia, the history of the New World and the Old, the Spanish language, and the town of Bernalillo. Any errors that survived their careful readings are the author's. Thanks to Erwin Bush for exploring Bernalillo with me, to my agent Dominick Abel, and my editor at Signet, Genny Ostertag. Thanks, too, to Robyn Mundy and David Holtby at the University of New Mexico Press and to Gérard Kosicki for making this edition such a beautiful book.

I am deeply grateful to Jerome Aragon for sharing his family's fascinating story.

I cared for you in the desert,
in the land of burning heat.

Hosea 13:5

CHAPTER ONE

During the break before summer session Claire Reynier walked across the University of New Mexico campus enjoying the quiet time when the students were gone and the campus reverted to the staff. With no students and backpacks to dodge, Smith Plaza felt larger. It was noon and the sun was directly overhead. The longest shadows she cast were the half moon beneath her visor and the darkness under her feet that made her feel there was another Claire, a reverse Claire, who extended into the ground and mirrored her footsteps from the other side. The sun warmed her shoulders and the top of her head. It wasn't searing hot yet, not so hot that she wanted to stay inside until dark, but hot enough to make her long for rain. As she approached Zimmerman Library, a massive pueblo–style building, her reflection was visible in the glass doors. In this light she saw more silver in her hair than gold. She looked slim enough in her pale summer dress, but knew she would look even slimmer if she straightened her back. She made the correction before she stepped into the library's familiar shelter.

I

She walked through the gallery which had an exhibition of Mexican photography from its sepia beginnings in the nineteenth century when itinerant photographers posed families in a stiff and formal way. She passed the nearly empty Anderson Reading Room. The young woman manning the information desk didn't glance up from her book. Claire crossed the hallway and went through the wrought iron gate into the Center for Southwest Research, grateful as always that she worked in such a beautiful place. She walked down the office corridor. Through the interior window that faced the hallway she was startled to see a woman she didn't know standing inside her office.

"Hello?" Claire asked, wondering whether the woman was a student. She wore a dark red skirt and top and platform shoes that brought her up to Claire's height. She had the slenderness of a stalk that swayed in the wind but the thick-soled shoes kept her grounded. Her hair was black and pinned up on top of her head with a spiky plastic clip. Her eyes were large and amber colored. The skirt was slinky and calf length. Her matching T–shirt had a golden butterfly embroidered across the bodice. The woman had a delicate, exotic quality Claire was unable to place. Her looks could have been Hispanic, Native American, East Indian, Middle Eastern, Asian or a mixture of any of them.

"Are you Claire Reynier?" she asked.

"I am."

"My name is Isabel Santos." She extended a hand with rings embellishing nearly every finger.

Claire shook her hand, then circled her desk and sat down behind it motioning for her visitor to do the same.

Isabel went to the visitor's chair and perched on the edge. "A woman at the Bernalillo Historical Society referred me to you. She said you were an expert on old documents."

"May Brennan?" Claire asked.

"That's her. I moved back from California to the family home in Bernalillo this spring. One of the bricks in the floor was loose. I tripped on it when I got up last night to go to the bathroom and I pulled it out. I was digging out the sand to make more room for the brick when I found something."

Claire knew that brick floors were often laid on a foundation of sand in New Mexico houses. "What?" she asked.

"An old wooden cross with a hole in the bottom. I picked it up and a rolled up piece of paper fell out. The cross had been hollowed out so the paper could fit inside." Isabel had a red suede purse dangling by a strap from her shoulder. She opened it and removed a piece of paper.

The archivist in Claire noticed that the paper was white and crisp and new. "Is that what you found?" she asked doubting that there could be anything of value to the center on such white paper.

"No," Isabel replied. "The paper I found was really old and dry. I didn't want to mess it up by moving it around so I copied what it said."

She handed over the paper. Up close Claire could see that it had blue notebook lines and that the writing on it was as round and symmetrical as a schoolgirl's.

"*Todo sta de arriva abasho,*" she read. "*El fuego o el garrote. Dame el fuego. Adonay es mi dio.*"

"Is that some kind of old Spanish like Castilian?" Isabel asked. She spoke the word Castilian with a contemptuous lisp then laughed. To speak Castilian Spanish was considered arrogant in parts of New Mexico.

"It might be an archaic form of Spanish," Claire said. "*Arriva* could be a variant of *arriba*. *Abasho* could be a variant of *abajo*."

"As in 'everything is up and down'?" Isabel asked.

"Or 'upside–down'," Claire said.

"And *garrote*? What does that mean?"

It was Claire's nature and her job to be careful, but she knew all too well what *garrote* meant. In English or in Spanish it was an instrument used to strangle people during the Inquisition. *El garrote* was considered kinder than *el fuego*— "the fire"—being burned at the stake. The distinction had always seemed a subtle one. In either case the victim ended up dead. She explained to Isabel what *el garrote* meant.

"And *Adonay*? What is that?" Isabel asked.

"The Spanish version of the Hebrew word for God," Claire said. "Are you sure it said *dio* and not *dios*?"

"Yes. That seemed weird to me because we always say *dios.*"

"The Spanish Jews said *dio*; for them there was only one God."

"You think this was written by a Jew?" Isabel said, balancing on the edge of her chair.

Yes, was Claire's thought, but the archivist's response was, "It could have been. The language could be Ladino, the language used by the Sephardic Jews, which was a combination of Spanish, Arabic and Hebrew. These words appear to have been written by a Jew who faced the Inquisition."

"Was the Inquisition practiced here?"

"No one was actually killed in New Mexico, but people were garroted and burned at the stake in South America and Old Mexico, where the Inquisition was practiced until the wars of independence."

"There was a Marrano in our house." Isabel laughed, puckering her lips like she had bitten into a piece of rancid meat.

Literally, Marrano meant swine, but it was also a word used to describe Jews who converted to Catholicism during the Inquisition. The more polite word was "converso".

"If this was written by a Marrano then why was it hidden inside a cross?" Isabel asked.

"It's possible the person who wrote it thought a cross was the last place anyone would look or the author was trying to pass as a Catholic. Is your family Catholic?"

"Are you kidding?" Isabel said. "Is the Pope? We have the last name of the saints. My brother's first name is Jesus."

Pronounced "haysoos", it wasn't such an unusual name in Spanish. "How long has your family had the house?" Claire asked.

"Forever. My grandmother grew up there."

"An ancestor might have buried the cross under the floor."

"My ancestors were not Jewish."

"Was the document signed?" Claire asked.

"Yes. It was signed Joaquín."

Joaquín was a common enough name in the Spanish speaking world, but the further back one went in the New World the fewer Joaquíns there were until the number became miniscule and then there were none. One of them once made the statement that the number of real Christians in the New World could be counted on the fingers of one hand. If that Joaquín had written and signed this document it would be extremely valuable. The story of how it got to New Mexico and under the bricks in Isabel Santos's floor could be written later. The most important thing at this point would be to safeguard the document. Exposing it to the light after years in darkness could be ruinous.

"I'll need to see it to be sure," Claire said, "but it could be a document of enormous historical significance. If it is, we would love to have it here in the center." She didn't think she was being unduly acquisitive. The center had the facilities to preserve it and make it available to scholars.

"Who is this Joaquín?" Isabel asked.

"There was a Jewish mystic named Joaquín Rodriguez who was killed by the Inquisition in Mexico City in the late sixteenth century."

"If the paper is that old, it would be *very* valuable, wouldn't it?"

"It could be," Claire admitted, knowing that much as she would love to have it in the center there were other institutions and collectors who could pay more.

"I'll have to think about it," Isabel said putting her hands on the edge of her chair as if preparing to push off.

"Of course," Claire replied, reluctant to see her leave. "The document could be fugitive to light. You should get it in a controlled environment as soon as possible. We have the optimum conditions here and would be happy to preserve it and protect it until you decide what to do."

"I'll get back to you, okay?" Isabel stood up wobbling for a second before she found her balance on the platform shoes.

"I can come out to your house and take a look at it if you like," Claire said. She didn't want Isabel to leave the center, but didn't know how to keep her. As a mother of two grown children she saw a fragility in Isabel that made one want to shelter her as well as a determination to go her own way that would make mothering difficult.

"Okay. I'll let you know what my family says. Thanks for talking to me." Isabel left without reclaiming her note.

Claire watched her walk away swinging her purse with a long, bare arm. It seemed to pick up momentum as she walked.

Once Isabel had disappeared around the corner, Claire made a copy of the note and locked the original in the bottom drawer of her desk. Then she walked down the corridor in the other direction, noticing as she passed several empty offices that most of her coworkers were out. She was pleased when she got to Celia Alegria's and found her working on her computer. Celia, who was determined not to let the library turn her into a brown bird, often wore velvet to work. It was too hot for velvet and today she had on a yellow linen dress and a necklace that was a string of turquoise birds in flight. All the color at CSWR seemed to be concentrated in Celia's office. The folk art posters on the wall and the shrine to Frida Kahlo on her bookshelf made the point that she remained in touch with her Mexican heritage.

Claire stepped into her office and shut the door behind her.

"Harrison?" Celia asked, looking up from the computer and raising her eyes to the ceiling. Harrison Hough, their prickly boss, was a frequent source of annoyance. Closing the door was a signal that she expected Claire to complain about him.

"Not this time," Claire said, handing her the copy of Isabel's note. "What do you make of this?"

Although Spanish language and history had long been a subject of interest to Claire, Celia had a Ph.D. in history and had studied in Mexico and Spain. "The language is Ladino. I'd say it was written by a Jew who faced the Inquisition, but that person didn't write it on twenty-first century notebook paper," Celia said.

"A woman named Isabel Santos brought it to my office referred to me by May Brennan of the Bernalillo Historical Society. She claims she found the original document inside a cross buried beneath a brick in the floor of her house in Bernalillo."

"Have you seen the original?"

"No. Is there any way of telling whether this was written in the New World or the Old World by the content?"

Celia studied the note. "Not really. The Inquisition was practiced many places—Old Spain, New Spain, Peru, Colombia. The Spaniards didn't just kill Jews either. They killed Muslims, Protestants, even Catholics who had strayed. In theory the Holy Office of the Inquisition punished lapsed Catholics. In 1492, all the infidels had to convert to Catholicism or leave. Some Jews and Muslims converted but with varying degrees of conviction. Supposedly, converso families weren't allowed to emigrate to the New World, but some did. The ones who went on practicing Judaism in secret became known as crypto Jews. There is no record of anyone ever being killed for practicing Judaism in New Mexico. We have that distinction. But crypto Jews were not allowed to own property or to hold water rights here. If they were found out they would lose their water rights which could be a death sentence."

"What if the document was signed Joaquín?"

"Just Joaquín?"

"That's what Isabel said."

"Well, if it was signed 'Joaquín Rodriguez' I'd say it was written by the Jewish mystic who was killed by the Inquisition in Mexico City in 1596 except that he wasn't burned at the stake. He was garroted. His death is well documented. The Spaniards kept detailed records of everything they did. If it's just Joaquín, I don't know. There could have been other Joaquíns who were burned at the stake during the Inquisition. Supposedly Joaquín Rodriguez converted and was saved from the fire, but his sister Raquel was incinerated. She went to her death screaming at her Inquisitors. She was even more passionate about her *dio* than Joaquín was. And he was pretty passionate. Often crypto Jews were not circumcised as infants because that gave them away. When Joaquín was fifteen he circumcised himself with a pair of scissors in the Rio de los Remedios." Celia grimaced at the thought. "If you had a choice, which would you choose? The fire or the garrote?"

"Does it matter? Either way you're dead."

"Most people preferred strangulation when given a choice. Burning takes longer and is more painful. The special collections library at Berkeley recently acquired a treasure trove of Inquisition documents, the largest collection of Mexican Inquisition papers in this country. The fact that this person chose the fire might indicate that this wasn't written by Joaquín Rodriguez. There are some scholars who could help you. Peter Beck at Berkeley is a leading scholar of the Mexican Inquisition. Your friend August Stevenson in Santa Fe authenticated the documents for Berkeley. But you'd have to have the original before you could establish anything definitive."

"I hope I can get it," Claire said.

"Of course you can. What was this doing buried under the floor of a house in Bernalillo?"

"I don't know."

"It could have been there for hundreds of years. It could also have been put there more recently. If you bring it to the center, Harrison will want to establish for sure that it wasn't stolen. You know Harrison." She rolled her eyes again. "Have you said anything to him yet?"

"Not yet."

"It might be better to wait until you actually have the document in hand. Once Harrison hears about it, he'll get greedy.

You won't have any peace until he has it in his fingers. There's no guarantee we're going to get it, is there?"

"None," Claire admitted. "Isabel said the family has been here a long time. I'm hoping a state sponsored library will appeal to them."

"It might," Celia said. Her silver bracelets clinked as she rubbed her fingers together in the universal symbol of greed. "But money might appeal to them even more. There are plenty of places able to raise more money than we can. Berkeley has deep pockets. We'd lose but it would be fun to see Harrison get into a pissing contest with them."

"Even if the document isn't originally from Bernalillo, it was found there, which makes it in some way a part of New Mexico history. The center is where it belongs," Claire protested.

"You're right," Celia agreed.

"It would be good for the center. It would be good for New Mexico."

"It would be good for you," Celia said getting up and giving her friend a hug.

chapter two

 The next day Claire had a luncheon to attend in Santa Fe. She called August Stevenson and asked if she could stop by and see him afterwards.

"Of course," he replied. "I'd be delighted."

It was the response she expected, but she still enjoyed hearing it. August had a distinguished career in document verification in New York City before moving to Santa Fe, supposedly to retire. He was well into his seventies now, but as far as Claire could tell he'd barely slowed down. Instead of documents finding their way to him in New York City, they found their way to him in Santa Fe. August had helped her before with an important document. She respected his expertise and trusted his discretion.

He lived a few blocks from the Plaza in a quiet neighborhood that tourists rarely visited. After her luncheon Claire drove there and parked in front of August's small brick house. It took him a long time to answer the doorbell, but she knew he was on his way when she heard the shuffle of slippers against the wooden floor.

"Claire, my dear," he said swinging open the door,

staring at her through the thick lenses of his glasses and giving her the impression that he was peering out through the water of an aquarium. "Very good to see you."

"Good to see you, August."

"Come in."

He turned and shuffled down the hallway with Claire following him. His broad, hunched back and slow movements reminded her of a tortoise. When they reached his office, he lowered himself into a leather desk chair. Claire sat in an armchair.

"How are you?" she asked.

"All the better for seeing you. And how are things at the library?"

"Good," Claire said. They had more to say about their work than about their personal lives, so she got to the point. "I just came across a very interesting document I'd like to ask you about. A woman named Isabel Santos who lives in Bernalillo found it under her brick floor. May Brennan referred her to me."

"And how is May?" August asked. "I hear she is getting a divorce."

"It happens to the best of us," Claire said. "May will get over it sooner or later. Isabel didn't actually bring me the document, but she wrote down what it said."

August sniffed with contempt at the photocopy Claire presented. "Well that and four dollars will get you a cup of coffee at Starbucks. You know I rely on quality of paper and ink to establish the age of a document and on writing style to establish authenticity." Claire had the sense that he was pulling up his tortoise shell and retreating inside. "This looks like it was written by a schoolgirl."

"I know," she soothed. "Of course you need the original

document to come up with anything definitive, but in this case the content is so unusual I thought it might provide some clues." Claire didn't want to tip her hand by telling him she knew he had authenticated Inquisition documents.

He held the paper at arm's length trying to find the right perspective through the thick lenses. He pushed it away, pulled it close, scrunched up his forehead and studied it for some time before he said, "The content suggests it was written by a Jew who faced the Inquisition. Which Jew, which Inquisition, I couldn't say. A few years ago I examined some documents for UC Berkeley that involved the Mexican Inquisition. The documents were in private hands and Berkeley wanted to be sure they were authentic before purchasing them. The Spanish kept impeccable records, although perhaps they shouldn't have. The Inquisition was a despicable affair, one of the most despicable affairs in a long human history of despicable behavior. Humans are monstrously cruel creatures. Some people were burned at the stake in Mexico, the most famous of whom is Raquel Rodriguez, who remained a fervent Judaizer up until the moment she was consumed by the flames. If there really is an original document and it was written by Raquel Rodriguez . . ." He put the paper down and stared at Claire through the deep water lenses. "Well, that would be a find indeed."

"Isabel said it was signed 'Joaquín'."

"Just 'Joaquín'?"

"That's what she said."

"Ah, to have the original in my hands." August thumped his desk in frustration. "Raquel had a brother, a Jewish mystic named Joaquín, who was garroted."

Claire knew all this but she kept quiet waiting to see in what direction August's thoughts would lead him.

"I authenticated the document that described his execution. He converted at the last minute and was given the favor of being garroted."

"Isabel told me that she found the document inside a hollowed-out wooden cross."

"I suppose it's possible that the document was concealed in a cross that ended up in New Mexico. It may have been written on handmade paper imported from Europe, which could survive for hundreds of years in New Mexico's dry climate. The Inquisition was heating up in Mexico City at the end of the sixteenth century. It has long been believed that some Jews whose names appeared on the Inquisition lists came north with Don Juan de Oñate's expedition in fifteen ninety-eight. Few questions were asked of anyone willing to make the arduous journey into unknown territory. There are samples of both Joaquín and Raquel's handwriting extant. It would be very easy to establish if he wrote these words if only I could see the original."

"Isabel said she would get back to me."

"Keep after her. This could be a very important find. I'd hate to see it go to some wealthy collector or to Berkeley. You, of course, have many years to make wonderful discoveries. But me?" The slowness of his shrug demonstrated the weight the carapace on his back had become.

After she left August's house Claire negotiated her way across The City Different in her pickup truck. She owned a truck because she needed one to transport books, but it also made a statement about the kind of strong and adventuresome person she was—or wished to be. Santa Fe was founded in

1610 on the model of a Spanish colonial city with streets radiating from a central plaza and a cathedral a few blocks away. It was to be expected that the Spanish would build a city resembling the ones they came from. What always surprised Claire was that they would cross an ocean and find a place so similar geographically to the one they had left behind. History was never very far away in New Mexico, which was one of the things she liked about it. She enjoyed the sensation of moving from one century to another.

On her way out of town she stopped at twenty-first century Wild Oats to buy granola and bagels. As she checked out she noticed the clock on the wall said four-fifteen. Wondering whether there was any need to return to her office at CSWR at this point or to just go home, she checked her voice mail from the cell phone in her truck. Talking on a cell phone was a private matter for Claire. She wasn't a person to walk up and down the aisles discussing what to buy for dinner. Besides, she had no one to discuss dinner with. She found a message from Isabel Santos on her voice mail saying, "I want to talk to you again. I'll be in Albuquerque tomorrow and will stop by your office."

Claire left the parking lot and drove down St. Francis Drive to the interstate. It wasn't long before she was out of the city and into the wide open spaces of I-25. She saw a cluster of lenticular clouds hanging over the Ortiz Mountains and one had been twisted into the perfect symmetry of a corkscrew. She inserted a cassette of the Indian rock group Red Thunder into her tape deck. The backdrop of drums and chanting and the ease of the drive left her mind free to wander. It headed back to Southern Europe and Northern Africa, the region that was the source of the Inquisition. There was a time when Muslims, Jews and Catholics lived in harmony, but that ended and the Inquisition began, forcing Jews and Muslims to convert, leave the Iberian Peninsula, or be persecuted.

Claire had taken a semester off when she was in college and spent some time traveling through Spain and Morocco with an Italian man named Pietro Antonelli in a Volkswagen van that broke down in every country they visited. She had recently tracked Pietro down on the Internet to the University of Florence, where he taught. Now that she had his E-mail address, she had been composing E-mails in her mind, but she hadn't arrived at the perfect phrasing yet. To help the process she popped out Red Thunder and inserted Andrea Bocelli. Listening to the Italian tenor and composing an E-mail to Pietro made the time pass quickly. When she reached the Bernalillo exit, a few miles north of Albuquerque, she turned off, thinking she might not have to wait until tomorrow to speak to Isabel.

She stopped at a convenience store on Route 44, went to the pay phone and flipped through the phone book that dangled beneath the stand. If Isabel had recently returned to Bernalillo her phone number wouldn't be listed yet. But Claire expected there to be other listings for Santos and she found three: Chuy and Tey in Bernalillo and Manuel in Placitas. She called the two in Bernalillo, getting no answer at one and voice mail at the other. She wrote down the addresses then went inside the store to ask the clerk for directions.

The young woman with a mane of curly brown hair was busy talking on the phone. Claire stood in front of the counter feeling invisible while she waited for the conversation to end. Realizing that being empty handed offered no inducement, she picked up a newspaper and placed it on the counter. The clerk hung up. Claire paid for the newspaper and asked if she knew where either address was. She didn't know Mejia Street where Tey lived, but directed Claire to Calle Luna, the address for Chuy.

"Thanks," Claire said.

"Sure," the girl replied picking up the phone again.

Claire drove south through Bernalillo on Camino del Pueblo looking for the turnoff that led to Calle Luna. The Sandia Mountains in the east were the color of slate mirroring the color of the clouds that had formed over the West Mesa. It was the time of year when clouds began to build up late in the day, but rain rarely fell until later in the summer. Claire thought of this as the waiting-for-rain season, when the earth seemed to be holding its breath in parched anticipation. Camino del Pueblo was once El Camino Real, the royal road that led from Mexico City to Santa Fe, traversed by a long line of oxcarts, horses, settlers, friars and conquistadors, traversed now by trucks and motorcycles and SUVs. The road was lined with churches, a courthouse, a hardware store, a bar, restaurants and storefronts, but a few blocks behind it were quiet streets and open fields. Claire turned off Camino del Pueblo and followed the directions to 625 Calle Luna.

The street ended in a cul-de-sac beside an irrigation ditch. As Claire turned the corner she saw that the cul-de-sac was filled with one ambulance and a swarm of white and brown Sandoval County Sheriff's Department cars. She hoped that 625 wouldn't turn out to mark the end of Calle Luna, but as she followed the numbers down the street she had the ominous sensation that it would.

CHAPTER THREE

Claire saw the number 625 set in tile in an adobe wall, parked in front of it and got out of her truck. The house was in the northern New Mexico style with a pitched tin roof ending in a porch. The walls hadn't been stuccoed and she could see straw sticking out of the adobe. The yard was full of police officers. One of them saw her and walked down the path.

"Can I help you, ma'am?" he asked. He was young with a stocky build and a thick black mustache. He had a tough–guy appearance but his manner was deferential. "I'm Detective Jimmy Romero."

"Is this 625 Calle Luna?" Claire asked, thinking it was a stupid question but not knowing what else to say.

"Yes. And who is it that you're looking for?"

"Isabel Santos."

"You mind telling me why?"

"My name is Claire Reynier. I work at the Center for Southwest Research at UNM. I met Isabel when she came to see me yesterday. She found a document buried under the house that she thought might be of interest to the center."

"What kind of a document was that?"

"A historical document. You need to tell me. Has something happened to her?"

"The house was robbed and she . . . well . . . Isabel Santos is dead."

"Oh, no." She turned toward the house. It had a beautiful, verdant setting but it was an unpretentious house. "What would anybody want to steal from here?"

"We don't know yet," Detective Romero answered.

"I need to speak to the person in charge of the investigation," Claire said. "There was a phone call on my voice mail from Isabel this afternoon."

"What did she say?"

"That she wanted to see me tomorrow."

"Do you know what time that call was made?"

"I left my office at eleven. It was sometime after that. The time will show up on my caller ID."

Detective Romero asked her wait in the yard while he talked to the investigation commander. Claire sat down at a picnic table under a cottonwood tree, watching the activity going on around her but feeling detached and isolated from it by a bubble of shock. How could Isabel, so full of life and potential yesterday, be dead today? Detective Romero spoke to a police officer on the porch then went inside the house. A friendly black dog walked up and rested its nose in her lap while she scratched its head. The field around the house had been irrigated with water from the irrigation ditch and was green with alfalfa. Horses grazed at the far end.

A man stepped off the porch and walked over to Claire. His hair was streaked with gray and he had a middle-aged spread. He wore jeans and a T-shirt decorated with the feathered logo of Santa Ana Star Casino. His hand had the curve of a container. Today it held a Dr. Pepper.

"I'm Chuy Santos," he said. "Isabel's brother." Up close his eyes were large and full of pain.

"Claire Reynier," she replied. "I am so sorry to hear about Isabel. I can't believe anything like this could happen to her. She was such a bright spirit."

"Are you a friend of hers?"

"No. I just met her. I'm an archivist at UNM. She came to see me about a document she found. Is this where she was living?"

"Yes."

"Is it your house?"

"It belongs to all of us." Chuy sat down on the bench on the other side of the picnic table. The dog went to him and he patted its head. "What document are you talking about?"

Claire wondered if she would betray a confidence by telling him, but decided that when a document was found in a house that belonged to a family the document belonged to the family. She pulled Isabel's note from her purse and showed it to Chuy. "She didn't actually show me the document, but she wrote down what it said and brought it to me."

Chuy took a sip of his Dr. Pepper and studied the document. "That's my sister's handwriting, but I never saw anything like this anywhere."

"She said she was going to discuss it with the family."

"She didn't discuss it with me," Chuy said, "and I'm her family. My sister went to California to get away from all of us. She comes back, starts getting her shit together. Now this . . ."

Paramedics came out of the house bearing a body on a stretcher. They loaded it into the ambulance and drove away. A man who left the house with them came over to the picnic table. He wore slacks with a sharp crease and a white shirt with sleeves so carefully rolled they appeared to be creased, too. His hair was black. He was slim and rather elegant, Claire thought, wondering if he might be the investigation commander.

"Hey, bro," Chuy said.

The man put his hand on Chuy's shoulder and Chuy gripped it with rough, callused fingers.

"This is my brother Manuel. Damn, I forgot your name already," he said to Claire. "I'm not playing with a full deck right now."

"I'm Claire Reynier. I met Isabel yesterday. I feel terrible about this," she said.

"It sucks, don't it?" Chuy said, taking a loud sip from his Dr. Pepper. It seemed to Claire that he became coarser after his brother appeared, but Manuel was smooth enough to make most people seem coarse in comparison. She placed him as the eldest sibling with Chuy in the middle and Isabel as the youngest. He had her amber eyes, although they lacked her warmth. His eyes were on remote. The dog wagged his tail but stayed away from the creases in Manuel's pants.

"Thank you for your concern," he replied.

"Claire here said Isabel found a paper in the house. She wrote down what it said and took it to UNM."

"Is this it?" he asked, taking the paper and reading it.

"Yes," she said.

"And how do you interpret this?" Manuel asked, handing the paper back.

"It appears to be something written by a Jew during the Inquisition."

"*Hijole*," said Chuy.

"Where did she say she found it?"

"She said there was a loose brick in the floor. She pulled it out and found a wooden cross buried in the sand with the document inside. If I saw the original document it would be easier for me to judge how authentic it was, but she didn't bring it to the library."

"I didn't see anything like that in the house, did you?" Chuy asked. "It's a mess in there. Stuff was thrown everywhere."

"Could you tell if anything is missing?" Claire asked.

"The TV, the stereo, stuff like that," Chuy said.

"It was a local kid," Manuel said, "looking for drugs and guns. My sister walked in and surprised the thief. The most dangerous part of a robbery is interrupting one."

Detective Romero stepped out of the house and motioned to Claire. "Lieutenant Kearns will see you now," he said.

chapter four

Claire left the Santos brothers at the picnic table and went to talk to the Lieutenant. He had a rumpled, jowly face, bristly reddish-brown hair and eyes the pale blue of an Eastern sky. Claire had been way off the mark when she thought the immaculate Manuel Santos was the investigator. Lieutenant Kearns's pants had never known a crease and his short sleeve shirt was wrinkled. His arms were thick with rusty hair.

"You wanted to talk to me?" he asked.

Claire handed him her card. "Isabel came to see me about a document she discovered in the house. I did some research and found out it could be quite valuable. She left a message on my voice mail today saying she wanted to see me. I stopped by this afternoon."

Lieutenant Kearns turned the card over his fingers. "Do you have any ID?" he asked.

In Claire's experience when a middle-aged woman was noticed at all her respectability was taken for granted, but she opened her purse and produced the driver's license and UNM card that proved her identity.

"Do you have a copy of the document?" Kearns asked.

"I have a copy that Isabel made in her own handwriting." Claire handed it to him.

"Have you seen the original?"

"No."

The Lieutenant frowned at the paper, squeezing a few more wrinkles into his forehead. "What does this mean?"

"I think it was written by a Jew about to be killed by the Inquisition."

"That would make it what? Three, four hundred years old?"

"If it is from the New World. If it's from Spain it could be even older."

"Could something like that survive for centuries?"

"Under the right conditions."

"Is there a market for it?" The Lieutenant squinted into the sun breaking through the late afternoon clouds.

"Yes, but I'd have to do more research to tell you exactly what that is and I'd need to see the original. Isabel told me it was inside a wooden cross she found beneath the brick floor. Did you see a wooden cross in the house or an old document?"

"No, but we weren't exactly looking for a cross or an old document. We're doing a room-to-room, plain view search. It appears to be the typical crime scene of someone lookin' for something they could use or fence quick—drugs, guns, jewelry, money, cell phones, VCRs, stuff like that. We see this kind of robbery every day in Sandoval County. It can turn tragic if the owner has the misfortune of walking in on the perp."

In Claire's experience people were also capable of killing for rare and valuable objects not so easy to fence. She knew that once she got back to her office and the shock of Isabel's death wore off, guilt that she had not gotten here sooner would fill the chasm created by the death. To stumble on the crime scene was deeply disturbing, but she would feel worse if she left here without taking advantage of the opportunity being offered.

"The document Isabel described could be very valuable to the family and to historians," she said. "If it is here, it needs to be preserved. I might be able to help your investigation by looking through the house. I may be able to pinpoint where she found it."

Lieutenant Kearns leaned against the wall and studied her. Claire supposed he wondered if she really could be useful to his investigation or if she had some other agenda for getting inside the house.

"I am an archivist," she added. "I work with historical documents."

"I need to go inside and make a few calls," Kearns said.

Claire waited, wondering just whom he was calling. A superior? Someone he knew at UNM? The campus police? She hoped the phone calls wouldn't lead to Harrison, her boss. The last thing she'd want him to know was that she was at the scene of a criminal investigation.

Kearns came back outside. "All right. You may look, but that's it, and you've got to cover up your hands and feet."

He produced a pair of plastic booties and plastic gloves and Claire put them on. He opened the door and they stepped into darkness and chaos. Policemen in brown uniforms swarmed all over the living room. When they saw Claire the buzzing stopped. Kearns explained why she was there and they resumed their investigation. Sofa pillows had been tossed on the brick floor, drawers were emptied and the contents spilled out, an end table was tipped on its side, a lamp smashed. The wreckage struck Claire as the work of a crazed or reckless thief or someone trying to create that impression. Beside a heavy wooden table there was an outline on the floor where the body had been. The red suede bag lay within the outline. The image of a single platform shoe tipped on its side jumped out at her from the clutter, an image likely to return in the middle of the night. Claire saw no religious objects in the room: no crosses, milagros, or images of the saints.

"Isabel told me she tripped over the brick on her way to the bathroom," Claire said. "May I?"

"Go ahead."

She followed the hallway leading to the bathroom and the bedroom. The bathroom seemed untouched but the bedroom was as chaotic as the living room. Pillow cases had been ripped from the pillows. A shawl had fallen or been tossed from the bed to the floor. The drawers and the closet had been ransacked.

"Petty thieves follow a pattern. They go to the closets and bedside drawers first looking for guns," Lieutenant Kearns said.

The destructiveness of the theft made Claire despair about the condition of the document if it was ever found. Movement was one antidote to depression and she made herself start at the bed and follow the path Isabel would have taken to the bathroom. All the bricks she saw were in place, but the shawl concealed part of the path. It was a red Spanish shawl with deep fringe as vivid as Isabel herself.

"Could we move this?" Claire asked.

Lieutenant Kearns called in Detective Romero, who had put on plastic gloves. He gathered up the shawl with a movement as gentle as an embrace and put it on the bed. As the bricks came into view, Claire felt the thrill of discovery. The brick that Isabel had moved was obvious. The others were embedded in sand, but one was framed by the dark outline of space.

"That must be it," Claire cried, pointing toward the brick.

Detective Romero knelt down, inserted the blade of his pocket knife into the crevice and began working the brick out of its space. Claire's hopes were that the cross and document would surface beneath the brick. She wanted to pace away her anxiety while Romero worked, but she forced herself to stand still clenching her hands into fists. Eventually he wiggled the brick out of its space. The sand had settled and formed a pocket under the brick, but to Claire it was a void. The cross and the document were not there. She squeezed her fists tight and then she let go.

Romero placed the brick on the floor, then moved his hand around the edges of the void. "This pocket goes under other bricks," he said. "Do you want me to continue?"

"Yes," Kearns said.

The adjacent bricks were packed together. Romero began digging out the sand that separated them. It was slow, painstaking work. Claire understood why Isabel hadn't searched any further after she found the cross. She felt like sinking onto the bed, but forced herself to stand and watch. She was intrigued by Romero's absorption in his work. Lieutenant Kearns went back into the living room. Although that room bustled with police activity, Romero created an island of quiet around him. He moved with the precision of an archaeologist and Claire wondered if he'd had any training in that area. As the bricks came out he piled them on the floor. The pocket grew until it ended in a depression about two feet wide. Romero dusted his hand across the top of the sand to feel if anything else was buried without actually disturbing it. His hand felt something and he began to gently brush the sand aside to expose it. Claire had become as focused on his search as he was, wondering if the cross had slid under here. His movements were light as a feather as he brushed the sand. She held her breath while something began to emerge. As Romero continued brushing the sand aside, she could see that it wasn't the weathered wood of an old cross. It became a knob and then it turned into the joint of a finger. He brushed a little further and the shape of a skeletal hand, white and mournful as a pieta, appeared in the sand. For a moment he and Claire stared at each other stunned into silence. Then he stood up and called for Lieutenant Kearns.

"You'll wanna take a look at this," he said.

Kearns came back into the room holding a plastic evidence bag.

"I'll be damned," he said staring into the sand.

"You want me to continue?" Romero asked. "There could be a body attached to this."

"No. If those are old bones we need to call in the Office of the Medical Investigator's forensic anthropologists." He held up the evidence bag for Claire to see. "We found a cross."

It was about six inches long, weathered wood with a few specks of green paint.

"Where was it?" Claire asked.

"In the purse lying on the floor."

"The one inside the outline of the body?"

"Yes. The strap was over her shoulder. The purse must have slipped under her as she fell."

"She may have been trying to protect the cross," Claire said.

"Maybe," Kearns replied.

Claire wondered if Isabel had been planning to bring the cross to her at the center. She hesitated to ask the next question. "Was the document inside the cross?"

"No." The Lieutenant turned the bag upside down to show her the hollow in the bottom of the cross. There was room for a document, but the space was empty.

Her disappointment was balanced by the excitement of the hand under the floor. For the police that investigation was just beginning, but in her mind the two finds were linked. "It's possible that the document Isabel found belonged to this body," she said.

"You're getting ahead of yourself," Kearns replied. "We don't have a document and we don't have a body. All we have is the skeleton of a hand."

Claire knew she was about to be dismissed. The lieutenant extended his hand. "Thank you for your help," he said. "We'll call you."

"Please," Claire said.

Kearns asked Romero to escort Claire to her vehicle. They walked through the living room and back outside. The Santos brothers had gone to the far side of the house and were leaning against a truck talking to an elderly woman. Claire wanted to tell them about the hand beneath the floor, but that wasn't her job.

"Thanks for your help," Romero said, echoing his boss. He opened the door of her truck for her.

"Let me know what develops, please," she said.

"We will."

CHAPTER five

Claire drove down Calle Luna and reversed her path to Camino del Pueblo. From here she could see that the clouds on the West Mesa had darkened and thickened. Although they appeared to be heavy and pregnant with rain, she doubted it would come so soon. June was the waiting season, not the rainy season. She headed north, turned right, and got on the interstate again, relieved that the rush hour was over and traffic was relatively light. She felt too drained to deal with heavy traffic. She debated whether to go home but decided to return to her office, replay Isabel's message, and think about all that had transpired.

By the time she parked and went into the center, anyone who had been there during office hours had gone home. Her office was dark and, on the surface, exactly as she had left it at 11 a.m. She turned on the light and checked the caller ID screen. Isabel had called at one p.m. and the number she called from was on the screen. She compared it to the numbers she had written down and found it to be the one listed for Chuy in the phone book. Isabel had said her brother was named Jesus and Chuy could be a nickname for Jesus. Before replaying

Isabel's message, she turned off the light to sit in darkness. In Claire's experience dimming one sense heightened the others. Listening in the dark could make hearing more acute, but she heard nothing in Isabel's voice that she hadn't heard earlier. Isabel sounded eager but not anxious or frightened or threatened. She didn't mention the purse, or the document, or the cross.

As Claire played the message over and over in the darkness, Isabel assumed the hallucinatory vividness of a dream. Claire could almost smell the fragrance of her skin and hear the rustle of her skirt. She saw the platform shoes, the red purse, the golden butterfly embroidered on the T-shirt. She had a mother's sense that she should have kept Isabel from danger and couldn't stand being in her office another minute. But before she left she turned on the light and checked the drawer in her desk where she had put the original of Isabel's note. It was still locked. The note was in place. The copy was in the hands of the police. Even so, Claire made another copy and took it home, locking the original back in the drawer.

When she finally fell asleep that night she saw red and gray in her dreams: a red skirt, a skeletal hand, a gray cross, the dancing flames of an auto–de–fé. In the morning she found a sage stick and took it to work. She was sitting at her desk with the fragrant sage in her hand when Celia walked into the office.

"You look exhausted," Celia said.

"I am."

Celia took the sage stick from Claire and sniffed it. "What are you planning to do with this?"

"I'd like to burn it to exorcise the spirit of Isabel Santos from my office."

"I heard about her on the news this morning. The newscaster said she walked in on a robbery at her home."

"The house is a wreck," Claire replied.

Celia stopped her examination of the sage stick. "You *saw* it?"

"Isabel left a message on my voice mail that she wanted to talk to me. I went to her house on my way back from Santa Fe. The Sheriff's Department was all over the place. They let me in and I directed them to the loose brick where the cross must have been. A detective started digging and the skeleton of a hand appeared in the sand."

"Does that mean there's a body connected to the document?"

"I don't know if there is a body. Maybe it's only a hand. The investigation commander called in the OMI."

"Was the document found?"

"It hadn't been when I was there," Claire said. "They found the cross but the document wasn't inside. The house was such a wreck I hate to think about the shape it would be in if it was in the house."

"If," echoed Celia.

"If," repeated Claire.

Celia put the sage stick back on the desk. "If you burn this it will set off an alarm and alert Harrison. You don't want to tell him about Isabel Santos do you?"

"No. He'll think everything I touch here turns to murder."

"Was she a positive spirit?"

"Yes."

"Why not keep her spirit around? Maybe you'll learn something from it."

"Maybe," Claire said.

Celia said she had to be at a meeting and left. This was the first time since they'd met that Claire hadn't noticed what Celia wore.

32

She expected Lieutenant Kearns to get in touch with her but it was Detective Romero who called that afternoon. He said he wanted to meet her in her office as soon as possible. They made an appointment for early the following morning; she didn't want her coworkers or Harrison to see a policeman in her office.

When the detective arrived at 7 a.m. Claire was waiting at the Information Desk to let him in. Romero's tough looks reminded Claire that the boys who got in trouble when she was in high school often became cops later on, that there was a connection between the criminal and the cop, the suspect and the prosecutor, the hunted and the hunter.

"Thanks for meeting me, ma'am," he said.

It was only recently that Claire started being called ma'am, and she was amused by it. "You're welcome," she replied.

"This is such a beautiful building," Romero said looking up at the rows of vigas in the high ceiling of the great hall. "I took a few courses here after I got out of high school, but then I got married, had a kid, got a job. I used to think I'd like to be an archaeologist."

"You looked like one when you were searching in the sand."

"I went on a few digs, and I enjoyed it. Maybe I'll come back someday, finish up after I retire."

He was young to be thinking about retirement, but people with government jobs were people who were willing to put their futures on hold. The death of Isabel Santos made Claire doubt the wisdom of putting anything on hold. She walked Romero down the hall to her office, flipped on the light switch and chased the resident spirit away.

"Have you established what killed Isabel?" she asked.

"Apparently she tripped and fell—or was pushed—against a table. Her neck landed hard on the edge and ruptured an artery. That can happen if you hit it just right. The force of the fall and the state of the house indicate there was a struggle. A gang member named Tony Atencio who lives in the neighborhood and has been in trouble before was seen running down the ditch that afternoon. We brought him in for questioning. Can you tell me what time Isabel called you?"

Claire brought up that information on her caller ID screen and showed Romero that it came in at one p.m. She accessed the message for him and said, "Isabel doesn't sound distraught to me."

"She doesn't," Romero agreed.

"Do you know what time she was killed?"

"Chuy Santos called 911 at three–thirty to say he'd found the body. All we can say for sure is that she died sometime between one and three–thirty. According to the phone records you were the last person she called that day."

"Did you find the document anywhere?"

"No."

"Isabel must have told somebody else about it. I know she talked to May Brennan at the Bernalillo Historical Society; it was May who referred her to me. It's possible she gave Isabel some other names."

"We'll check it out," Detective Romero said. "We need the original of the words she wrote down for you."

Claire unlocked the drawer and handed the paper to him. He stared at it. "What is your interpretation of this?"

"The language is Ladino, an ancient combination of

Hebrew, Spanish and Arabic. My translation is 'Everything is upside–down. The garrote or the fire. Give me the fire. Adonay is my God.' I've shown a copy to an expert here and one in Santa Fe and the consensus is it was written by a Jew who faced the Inquisition in either the New World or the Old."

"My grandmother says Jews came to New Mexico in the old days. They kept to themselves and practiced old customs. They didn't eat pork but sometimes they slaughtered a pig and hung it outside the house so no one would suspect. As time went by they began to forget that the reason they kept the old ways was because they were Jews."

"Did you grow up in Bernalillo?"

"Yes. I've lived there all my life."

"Do you know the Santos family?"

"I know Isabel went to California. I know Chuy likes to gamble. I know Manuel is a lawyer who lives in Placitas. The Republican party is preparing to run him for the State House."

Claire hadn't heard that. "Tell me about the hand you found. Did it lead to a body?"

"Yes. The OMI forensic anthropologists dug it out. They can tell how long it was buried there."

"Was anything else found?"

"Just the skeleton."

"Would the OMI consider turning it over to the Smithsonian? They have the best resources for establishing how old it is and where it came from."

"Usually the OMI handles the old bones themselves. There'd have to be something special for them to call in the Smithsonian."

"The document Isabel found makes this case special."

"It might if we had a document," Romero pointed out.

"You could begin by asking the Smithsonian to examine and date the cross," Claire said. "I don't know of anyone in New Mexico with the ability to do that." She was trying to capture the interest of the archaeologist in Romero.

"I'll talk to Lieutenant Kearns about it," he said.

"Maybe the old bones can tell us something about the more recent death."

"Bones make good witnesses. They never lie. But I have to tell you that Tony Atencio is looking pretty good to us right now. We picked up some prints and fibers at the crime scene. We'll see if we can get a match."

It was eight when he left. Claire wondered if it was too early to call August but she went ahead knowing that most older people slept little and woke early.

He answered so quickly his hand might have been resting on the phone waiting for a call. "Claire," he said, clearing his throat with the hoarseness of a smoker, although he claimed he hadn't smoked for years. "How are you, my dear? Was that *your* Isabel Santos who was killed in Bernalillo?"

"I'm afraid so," Claire said.

"The news reports say that she walked in on a theft. Do you know what happened to your document?"

"Not yet."

"It wasn't in the house?"

"The police haven't found it."

"A robber would never know its worth. Could she have sold it before this happened?"

"It's possible, but who would she have sold it to?"

"Some rogue collector. UC Berkeley. Unlike other universities we know, Berkeley will do whatever it can to keep scholars happy." He cleared his throat again, more for effect than from necessity.

Claire had been thinking theft, but she supposed it was possible that Isabel had sold the document. If so the buyer should come forward. The money should have been deposited somewhere which would be easy for the police to establish.

"There's more," she said. "A skeleton was found under Isabel's house near where the cross and document were. The OMI's forensic anthropologists are investigating."

"That raises all sorts of intriguing possibilities especially if the skeleton brought the cross and document to Bernalillo."

"It does," Claire agreed. "Is there anything in the documents you verified that might be helpful to me or the investigators?"

"There's a lot about the persecution of the Rodriguez family. Whether it would be helpful or not, I don't know."

"Would you be willing to make copies of the relevant documents for me?"

"Of course. I'll put them in the mail today."

"Thank you," Claire said.

"My pleasure," August replied.

chapter six

The documents were waiting for Claire when she got home after work on Friday. Her house was stifling after baking in the sun all day. She let the cat out, turned on the cooler and microwaved a bowl of leftover pasta for dinner. Then she took August's documents outside to her courtyard. Her house had a small backyard with a long view across the city and the Rio Grande Valley to the West Mesa. The sunsets were a glorious play of shadow and light but the view could be too vast. Claire felt her thoughts might float into the far away spaces and never return. For concentration she preferred the enclosed space of her courtyard. There were times when she enjoyed hiding behind the courtyard's high walls which reminded her of a medieval cloister. She had a datura plant that had volunteered to live on one side of her courtyard. On the other she had planted an herb garden of rosemary, sage and oregano.

She sat down on the banco, opened August's package and found a note from him saying that he had spoken to the Inquisition scholar Peter Beck and that Beck doubted Joaquín Rodriguez had ever written the document Claire described.

According to Beck it was well documented that Joaquín Rodriguez had converted and been garroted. Claire returned August's note to the envelope. Just like a scholar, she thought, to deny the existence of something that might contradict his scholarship. She didn't know Peter Beck, but she knew other scholars and she knew how committed they became to the positions that earned them their reputation.

Having dispensed with scholars, Claire turned to the photocopies of the documents written in the ornate penmanship of the sixteenth century. Flowery language matched the elegant handwriting. Her Spanish was good enough for a short document but too laborious for a long one. Fortunately August had enclosed the translations he had used in his authentication process. Authenticity was established by dating the paper and the ink and by comparing these documents to other official documents. One needed to know the content to do an effective comparison. It was hard for Claire to imagine people spending their time faking Inquisition documents, but she knew that forgers would fake anything they thought they could sell.

As she read the translations Claire learned that there had been three Rodriguez siblings: Joaquín, Raquel, and a younger brother named Daniel. The records of the Inquisition of Joaquín and Raquel were enclosed. There was no record of Daniel's fate, leading Claire to wonder if he had escaped the Inquisition. Perhaps he had been a less fervent Jew or a more convincing Catholic. No Spaniard was allowed to emigrate to the New World without at least pretending to be a good Catholic. Some came with the hope that they could abandon the pretense as they moved further away from the Church.

As Claire read on she learned that the Rodriguez family was accused of Judaizing by a neighbor in Mexico City. Once people were accused the Inquisitors were quick to incarcerate them and confiscate their property. The only way the accused could save themselves was to convince the Holy Office of the Inquisition that they had repented and embraced the Church. Although they were both tortured on the rack, neither Raquel nor Joaquín repented. Both were convicted of apostasy and "relaxed to the secular arm," meaning they were turned over to the civil authorities for public execution. Raquel was burned alive at the stake.

Joaquín was accused of "making jokes about Our Lord Jesus Christ and insulting Our Lady." Although he was a baptized and confirmed Catholic, he reverted to his family's Jewish beliefs "like a dog who returns to his vomit."

Joaquín responded that he obeyed only the Law of Moses. His God "cares for me in the desert in the land of burning heat, and brings water, honey and oil from the rock. He will welcome me into heaven with strumming harp and clicking castanets. Starve me, break my body on the rack, but my faith remains gold in the treasure chest of my mind."

He was sentenced to be led "through the streets on a saddled horse with a crier telling of his crime." Someone in the crowd stepped forward and Joaquín spoke words that were interpreted as a conversion. When he arrived at the marketplace of San Hipólito, he was garroted until he died, and then his body was taken to the *quemadero*—the burning ground— put on the fire and burned to ashes.

Claire liked to believe the words *dame el fuego* were truly Joaquín's last words and wishes. The Joaquín she'd just read about wouldn't have converted out of fear of the fire. The elegant handwriting and the poetic language described a barbaric act, one of many that had been committed in the name of somebody's God.

The light had faded in the courtyard. Claire looked up and saw the red glow of the planet Mars hanging over the Rio Grande Valley. Tonight was the dark of the moon and there was nothing in the sky to diminish Mars's light. The red planet, considered the ruler of war, action and aggression, was at its closest point to earth in many years. Claire knew mankind was capable of vicious acts. However, blood spilled in the heat of passion and war, blood spilled over lust or fear or territory, was more understandable to her than blood spilled in a cold and calculated public execution. It took time for the Holy Office of the Inquisition to try and execute the lapsed Catholics. At any time in the long process the Inquisitors could have shown compassion and tolerance, but they never did. The Inquisition continued for centuries in the Old World and the New. In Claire's mind it was one of Christianity's darkest chapters. Her heart was with the passionate Joaquín Rodriguez who had wanted nothing more than to worship his God.

Her cat, Nemesis, startled her by jumping off the courtyard wall and landing in the herb garden, releasing the fragrance of oregano and rosemary. He meowed and rubbed against her legs indicating he wanted to go in.

Claire took him inside, sat down on the sofa in her living room, and turned on the light. Along with the Inquisition documents, August had sent copies of prints depicting the Inquisition of Raquel Rodriguez. With her breasts bare she was dragged in front of her black-robed, black-hatted Inquisitors. She was burned at the stake dressed in a *sambenito*, the yellow cloak and pointed hat Jews were forced to wear. The executioners' faces were well hidden by black hoods as they fed the flames. It was a horrifying image, not one Claire wanted to take to bed with her.

She looked through the documents again trying to find something in the elegant wording to erase the image of Raquel being burned at the stake, something trivial or stupid or even humorous. There was a kind of black humor in the wording of the documents. She found her diversion at the end of the "Inquisition Case of Joaquín Rodriguez" but it wasn't particularly humorous. The document concluded with a list of witnesses to the execution. She'd skipped over the list earlier thinking the names had no significance. This time, however, one name leapt out at her from the list, the name of Manuel Santos. He was one of the grim, sanctimonious, black-robed men who had watched Joaquín Rodriguez burn to cinder. And this was the name of Isabel Santos's brother.

Claire put down the document and began pacing from one end of her house to the other, wearing a path through the gray carpet. Nemesis watched from the sofa flicking his tail. She had wondered if the skeleton under the bricks was a Rodriguez who had come north with Joaquín's last words hidden inside a cross, possibly even with the Oñate expedition. It was a wise time for a Jew to escape Old Mexico. Claire had never considered that the bones could belong to an Inquisitor or the family of an Inquisitor. It was possible that Joaquín's encounter on the way to the stake was not as it was described in the Inquisition record. It was possible that the Church hadn't been able to convert Joaquín Rodriguez and had garroted him to save face, in which case the Inquisitors would not want his last words to be known. Had the record keepers, too compulsive to destroy them, buried them on the frontier?

Joaquín's Inquisition had happened over four hundred years ago. Would anyone care about having an Inquisitor as an ancestor at this point? Usually villainous relatives became less evil and more picturesque as time went by. But Inquisitors were a special class of evil. Did the Santos brothers know they were descended from one?

Those weren't thoughts that led to a good night's sleep, either. Claire went to her office and turned on the computer, thinking that writing her thoughts down could help her get rid of them. As she typed, she thought about the deep, dark evil of the Inquisition, an evil that had sprung from one of the most harmonious periods in history. Prior to the expulsion of the Muslims and Jews from Spain, the Iberian Peninsula had experienced an incredible flowering in the arts and the sciences. The scientific achievements and art that came from that period were remarkable. Claire thought about the symmetry and beauty of the Alhambra. She remembered sitting in the tiled courtyard with Pietro Antonelli, eating oranges, listening to the tinkling fountain.

If there was anything that could take her mind off the Santos and Rodriguez families, it would be Pietro. There was the risk that he wouldn't remember her or wouldn't answer her but if she didn't write him she would consider herself a coward. The dark of the moon marked the end of one phase, which led to the beginning of another. The red glow of Mars encouraged action. She typed the E-mail she had been composing in her head, trying to keep it brief and to the point. She told Pietro about her grown children—Eric was working in California, Robin studying in Boston—her divorce from Evan, her new life in Albuquerque. She said her work had recently caused her to think about Spain and North Africa and to wonder how he was. Before she could reconsider all the reasons why she shouldn't do what she wished to do, she typed his E-mail address and hit the send button.

chapter seven

She woke up early wondering what time it would be in Florence. Before she heated a bagel, made a cup of coffee, or drank a glass of orange juice, she checked her E-mail to see if there was a response. Nothing but the usual collection of porn and credit card offers. She began to realize how big a step she had taken with one small E-mail. Would it condemn her to look for an answer first thing in the morning, last thing at night and every hour in between? It wasn't the first time she felt like a teenager when it came to middle–aged romance. She had been in her late teens when she met Pietro, but in some ways she was more mature about love then than she was now, more secure about her looks and more optimistic about her ability to love and be loved back.

To convince herself that she wasn't obsessed with getting a reply, she decided to do some work while she was online. She poured a glass of juice, returned to the computer, went to the *Albuquerque Journal*'s website and typed in the name of Manuel Santos. The most recent article came up on the screen. Manuel made a statement expressing his sorrow at his sister's death and declaring that the state needed to get tougher on crime. Claire scrolled through earlier articles, learning that he had been in the news for years in a small way. He was a partner at a large, well-known law firm, and an active member of the Republican party. When a prominent Republican came to town, Manuel Santos was at the politician's side. When there was a fund–raiser for the party, Manuel was there. He was prodevelopment, anti–government spending, not particularly concerned with protecting the environment. There were photos with his attractive blonde wife and two adorable children. Manuel and his family lived in the hills of Placitas, where subdivisions with large lots looked down on the Interstate, the fast food strip of Route 44, the Santa Ana Casino, and the town of Bernalillo. Santos was the type of Republican with Hispanic roots that the party had been courting. Claire wondered if he'd also be willing to turn his back on his roots.

She checked her E-mail one more time, then logged off the Internet. After breakfast she called May Brennan.

"Hullo." May answered the phone in a voice that had a dull echo like it came from an emotional cellar.

She was getting a divorce and Claire knew what a miserable experience that was. She could also sympathize with any guilt felt about the death of Isabel Santos.

"May," she said. "This is Claire Reynier. Are you all right?"

"I've been better. And you?"

Been worse, Claire thought, remembering the dark days of her own divorce. "I'm all right, but I'm upset about the death of Isabel Santos."

"Me, too. I gave her your name. I gather she came to see you?"

"She did. Are you free for lunch?"

"I was planning to work at the Historical Society today, but I could take a break."

"The Range?" It was Bernalillo's best-known restaurant.

"Not there. Too busy. Too noisy. There's a new micro-brewery called Milagro on Route 44 just before the Santa Ana Casino. Can you meet me there at noon?"

"Okay," Claire said.

She allowed herself to check her E-mail just once more. Nothing from Pietro.

May was sitting at the table sipping a beer when Claire arrived at Milagro. The brewery was at ground level. The dining room was on the second floor. It was large and bright with brick walls painted white and an IMAX view of the Sandias. Cedar trunks went from the floor of the brewery to the roof, making the dining room feel like a tree house.

May was alone, but Claire had the sense that the gray moth of depression sat beside her, a companion that could drive all others away. Sometimes people had to isolate themselves in order to recover from a wound. Most people healed eventually and got back in circulation again. Reaching out to Pietro was a sign that Claire had finally healed from her divorce. But some people's wounds went too deep to ever heal. It was too soon to tell with May. Claire knew her ex-husband was a drinker who had been rude and abusive. He berated May publicly about her weight.

May wore no makeup, not even a touch of blush. The bright light at Milagro didn't flatter her pasty skin. Her hair was long and gray and piled carelessly on top of her head. She didn't get up when she saw Claire. Claire bent down and gave her a hug, noticing that May felt thick and lumpy as a pillow stuffed with straw.

"Good to see you, May," she said.

"You're looking well," May replied.

"Thanks. I feel good. There is life after divorce, you'll see."

May sighed. "I hope so. Going through it is a nightmare."

"Are you going to do all right financially?"

"Not if Rex can help it."

The waitress brought menus and took their drink orders. A designer beer for May. A lemonade for Claire.

"I feel terrible about Isabel Santos," Claire confided when they were alone again.

"Me, too."

"What do you think happened?"

"She walked in on a robbery by Tony Atencio, according to the Sandoval County Sheriff's Department."

"He's only a suspect. Nothing has been proven yet."

"No, but Tony's a gang member and he has been in trouble ever since he dropped out of middle school."

"Did you talk to the Sheriff's Department?"

"Yes. Lieutenant Kearns visited me. They found the call Isabel made to the Historical Society in her phone records. I told Kearns I had referred Isabel to you, but they already knew that you'd been involved."

"Was I the only person you referred Isabel to?"

May's eyeglasses dangled from a cord around her neck. She put them on and studied the menu before she answered Claire. "No. After she saw you she came to the Historical Society and told me you said the document was related to the Inquisition. She asked me if I thought it was valuable and I

47

mentioned Peter Beck and Warren Isles. Peter is an expert on the Inquisition. Warren is a collector in Santa Fe. I thought the document should go to the center, of course, but it was her choice."

"Do you know if she contacted them?"

"No. I gave her the names and numbers. I don't know what happened after that."

"Did she show you the document?"

"No." Her eyes went back to the menu. "The fish and chips are good. I'd recommend them."

"You're a historian. Weren't you curious? Didn't you want to see the original document? Weren't you tempted to go to her house?" Claire wasn't willing to let May slide by hiding behind the menu.

"I'm not as curious about things as I used to be." Her eyes—with or without the glasses—were dull as soot. "I tried to do you a favor, Claire. If you weren't interested in the document, you could have passed it on to someone who was."

"Actually I was very interested. The police haven't found the document in Isabel's house and I'm worried about what happened to it."

May wrapped her words in the ellipses of disdain. "Well . . . you know the Sandoval County Sheriff's Department . . ."

"Have you ever been to the Santos house?"

"Of course."

"Do you have any idea how old it is?"

This was a subject May was more willing to talk about. She became animated as she spoke, more like the woman Claire had known, a woman who was interested in her work and proud of her expertise. She put down the menu and let the glasses on the velvet cord drop back to her chest. "It's a hundred years old. The Santoses have been in Bernalillo since the very beginning. That property was once the family hacienda and they built and rebuilt on the same site. Lieutenant Kearns said a skeleton was found under the brick floor but he didn't know how old it was yet. It could be a family member. The first Manuel Santos came to New Mexico with Oñate's expedition. The family settled in San Juan but eventually ended up here although it isn't known exactly when. Records were destroyed during the Pueblo Revolt."

"The Spaniards all left then, didn't they?"

"Presumably. Although it's possible some of them made peace with the Indians and hid out until the area was conquered again. The Spaniards lived in widely separated family groups. It would have been hard to survive in Bernalillo in the early seventeenth century without getting along with the Indians. Sometimes Spaniards returned to their original homesteads."

"Have there been Manuel Santoses in Bernalillo since that time?"

"No. The name Manuel didn't get passed on in every generation. Most of the current Santoses aren't very interested in their own history. The latest Manuel hasn't given his son the name."

"There was an Inquisitor in Mexico City named Manuel Santos in the late sixteenth century."

"There was?" May seemed startled. "I didn't know that."

"August Stevenson gave me copies of Inquisition documents dated fifteen ninety-six with the name Manuel Santos on them."

"I'm sure Manuel would love to have it known that he was descended from an Inquisitor. That would really help his campaign. That and his gambling brother." May's voice was marbled with sarcasm but she laughed. It was the first laugh Claire had heard from her in a while. "But it's unlikely the two Manuel Santoses are related. An Inquisitor in Mexico City at that time would have been a powerful person. Why would someone with that kind of power leave for el Norte?"

"I don't know," Claire answered. "Have you ever come across evidence that any crypto Jews settled in Bernalillo? Maybe the conflict between the Rodriguez and Santos families played out again here."

"Nothing tangible," May said. "There is talk that the old ways endured in some families. That they burn candles in secret on Friday night, that they don't eat pork, that they sweep to the middle of the room. Even though I've lived here for forty years and know more about the history of the place than most people, I'm still considered an outsider. Anyone who secretly practices Judaism wouldn't admit it to me. I don't know why anybody needs to keep it a secret in this day and age, except that devout Catholics in the family would rather not know."

"Sometimes people fall into the habit of secrecy," Claire said. "And are unwilling or unable to stop."

"Sometimes," said May. She saw the waitress approaching. "If it's all the same to you I'd like to order now."

"All right."

May ordered the fish and chips. Claire got a duck and spinach salad. While they waited for the food to arrive, Claire's thoughts returned to Isabel Santos. "Did you know Isabel well?" she asked May.

"Not really. I saw her occasionally when she was growing up. She was a pretty girl with a lot of spirit. She had problems with drugs when she was younger. It caused a rift with her family, especially her brother Manuel, who's always been concerned about his image. She fell in love with an Anglo guy in California, but eventually she came back. It seemed like she'd made peace with her family and was settling down here."

"Are the parents still alive?"

"No. She was raised by her grandmother who lives in town."

When the lunch arrived the portions were enormous. May's plate overflowed with fries and fish. Although there was more than enough for two, she ate every bit.

chapter eight

After lunch Claire drove east on Route 44. The strip from Santa Ana Star Casino to I-25 was one of the places in New Mexico that combined the best of the past with the worst of the present. There was the casino, the convenience stores, the gas stations and fast food restaurants. But there was also the Coronado State Monument, a quarter mile away from the strip by road but much further than that in spirit.

It was one of Claire's favorite places in the state. Although named for a conquistador, it was more of a monument to the peaceful Kuaua people who lived on the banks of the Rio Grande when Coronado's expedition arrived in 1540. Most of the pueblo buildings were now in ruins. The kiva had been restored and could be entered by a wooden ladder, but the original frescoes had been removed and taken inside the Visitor's Center, a building designed by John Gaw Meem, the architect who designed the library where Claire worked. She felt a sense of shelter and timelessness in a Meem building. As she walked through the Visitor's Center she passed a child-sized suit of armor. Historical figures cast such long shadows it was surprising to be reminded that people were smaller 400 years ago. She went out the back door and followed the path around the pueblo ruins. The comments of the conquistadors were imprinted on sign posts stuck in the ground. In 1540 Pedro de Casteñada wrote about Indian women grinding corn, "A man sits at the door playing on a fife while they grind, moving the stones to the music and singing together." In 1610 Perez de Villagra wrote "They are quiet, peaceful people of good appearance and excellent physique, alert and intelligent. They live in complete equality, neither exercising authority nor demanding obedience."

Claire left the pueblo and walked down to the riverbank. Kuaua women were excellent swimmers and easily negotiated the treacherous currents of the river. In summer it had a wide, gentle flow and Claire liked to sit on the banks and watch it wander. She had a favorite spot sheltered by a cottonwood and she sat down there. The view here was south to the Sandias, not gentle mountains from any perspective, but from here they seemed even rockier and more jagged than they did from her house. Traffic crossed the bridge on Route 44, but the rippling water drowned out the sound. Coronado was close to the sprawl of Albuquerque, yet removed by the sense of being in another time.

Claire's mind regressed to the sixteenth century. It was 1598, almost 60 years after Coronado, before the Spaniards returned in any numbers. Settlers and friars came north with Oñate, and at some point after that a Manuel Santos settled in Bernalillo. Could it have been Manuel Santos, the Inquisitor, or a relative carrying a cross with the last words of Joaquín Rodriguez inside? What would that mean to the current Santos family?

As Claire watched the water, the sun beat down on her

back. From the beginning of civilization mystics had gone into the land of burning heat seeking enlightenment. She thought about Joaquín Rodriguez circumcising himself on the banks of the Rio de los Remedios—the courage, the pain, the sense of release and acceptance that could come from obeying a covenant of his God. His blood might have flowed into the water and blended into the current in the same way the waters of one river flowed into another when their paths came together, in the same way that people merged when they followed the same God.

Her thoughts moved on to May Brennan eating enough for two. She sympathized with her confusion and her pain about the divorce, but she wondered if despair was clouding her vision. She was bothered by the sense that May hadn't told her everything she knew. The May she knew would have insisted on seeing the original and gotten to Isabel's house even before Claire did. Claire stood up, took one last look at the free flowing river and walked back to her truck.

She took Camino del Pueblo south through Bernalillo and when she got to 711 Camino del Pueblo, the building that housed the Sheriff's Department and other county offices, she parked and went in. The building had been renovated and given a false front that reminded her of a western movie set.

She stopped at the front desk and asked for Detective Romero.

"He's not in," a soft-spoken policewoman replied. "Would you like to speak to Lieutenant Kearns?"

Claire had to say yes, although she doubted Lieutenant

Kearns would be as interested in the historical elements she'd uncovered as Detective Romero.

The woman rang Kearns and he walked down the hallway toward Claire. His clothes were very plain and rumpled. His posture had the weary droop of an old shoe.

"Ms. Reynier," he said, "what are you doing in Bernalillo?"

"I had lunch with May Brennan today. Then I went to Coronado Monument. It's one of my favorite places in New Mexico."

"Never had a chance to go there myself. One of these days. Well, come into my office."

Claire followed him into the office listening to the buzzing noises of a police station, thinking of it as the hive the force returned to at the end of the day weighted down with evidence found all over Sandoval County.

"Have you found the document yet?" she asked.

"Not yet."

"May told me you contacted her about the phone call Isabel Santos made to the Historical Society. She said she gave Isabel and you the names of Peter Beck and Warren Isles. Have you been in touch with them?"

"We're working on it," Kearns said, leaning against his desk and watching her with pale eyes, waiting to see where this was heading.

"It could be that Isabel contacted them, maybe even sold one of them the document." She didn't want to imply she could do his job better than Kearns could by suggesting that if there'd been a sale there could be a deposit somewhere.

"We haven't found any evidence to suggest she contacted anyone but you and May."

"It's such an important document. It's hard to imagine

any historian or collector hearing about it and not going to Isabel's house as soon as possible to see it. I did."

"We don't know that the experts May recommended ever heard about the document, but as I said we're working on it."

"Could you ask May if she contacted anyone?" Claire felt like a yappy little dog. She didn't like to think she was barking at Lieutenant Kearns's heels, but there was a lot at stake here, including her own reputation.

Kearns responded to her assertiveness by stepping behind his desk. "She says she didn't." The late afternoon sun followed him around the desk, beaming through the window, lighting up the rusty hair on his arms and turning the lines in his face from fissures to canyons.

Claire wondered if it was doing the same to her and stepped away from the light. "If a substantial amount of money was deposited in Isabel or the Santos brothers' accounts that would be on record, wouldn't it?"

"We have to have some reason to suspect there was a sale before we can go looking at people's bank accounts," Kearns said. "We don't even know that there was a document. May couldn't confirm it and you never actually saw it either, did you?"

"To me the content is confirmation. I don't see how Isabel could have made it up."

"It might be confirmation to a historian. A policeman needs something more tangible than a description," he reminded her.

"The cross could tell you more."

"We're investigating. The OMI identified the skeleton as a man, by the way. Sex is relatively easy for them to establish. For one thing a man's forehead has more slope than a woman's. It will take longer to determine the age and origin of the skeleton. It's old, but they don't know how old yet."

"I asked Detective Romero if the Smithsonian could be called in."

"They usually only participate in exceptional cases like ones that involve paleoindian artifacts."

"I think this is an exceptional case," Claire said. "I've been researching Inquisition documents and I discovered that there was an Inquisitor named Manuel Santos who witnessed the execution of Joaquín Rodriguez in Mexico City. May told me a Manuel Santos was part of Oñate's expedition and was one of the first Europeans to settle in Bernalillo."

"There could have been more than one Manuel Santos, no?"

"There were very few Europeans in the New World in the late sixteenth century." Claire persisted although she felt discouraged about convincing a man who worked in Bernalillo without ever visiting the Coronado Monument of the relevance of anything that happened here 400 years ago.

"Even if Manuel Santos's ancestor was an Inquisitor, that's not a crime at this point," Kearns said.

"It could have provided a motive for Isabel's death."

"To you Tony Atencio may be an uninteresting suspect but to us he's a gangbanger with a record. We found his prints in the house. He tried to sell Isabel's VCR to a buddy of his, and the buddy ratted on him. We had enough evidence to charge him with burglary and keep him in jail."

Claire thought she could be stating the obvious, but she did it anyway. "Maybe someone else fought with Isabel and she fell. Maybe Tony Atencio found her dead and took advantage of an opportunity."

"Maybe," Kearns said in a weary voice that lacked conviction. He turned to the window and asked, "You think it's going to rain?"

"No," Claire replied, recognizing the meaningless phrase that marked the end of the meeting.

"Either Detective Romero or I will be in touch," Kearns said.

chapter nine

Claire got in her truck and continued on through Bernalillo. She wasn't planning to go to Calle Luna, but when she saw the turn-off she acted on impulse and swung a right. The decision was made so quickly that she didn't have time to flick her turn signal. The driver of the car behind her leaned on his horn. His irate face was visible in her rear view mirror. She had learned much about the Santos family since the last time she was here. She wanted to look at Isabel's house again and see how it appeared through the lens of her new knowledge.

She wondered what it was like when Manuel Santos first came here with an oxcart full of possessions. There would have been paths but no roads. The only buildings were the Indian settlements along the Rio Grande. Before the river was dammed in the twentieth century the Bosque and the valley were a wide flood plain. Buildings had to be on higher ground to survive. Houses were built of native materials. The people were smaller then so the houses were constructed with low doors and no windows. Only the very well cared for buildings from that period survived. Mud houses were organic and eventually they sank back into the ground from which they had come. The first Santos dwelling might have stood on the spot of the present dwelling or it might not. It would be difficult to prove.

May might have more knowledge of the Santos family history than they did themselves but it wasn't so unusual for a family to lose touch with their own history. Genealogy was an interest that families drifted in and out of and that was partially a function of age. As people got older and concerned with their own mortality, they became more interested in their ancestors. Claire knew that the Reyniers had arrived in New Amsterdam in 1650 on a ship called the Gilded Otter. They had a French name but they traveled to the New World on a Dutch ship.

She turned onto Calle Luna. As she neared the cul-de-sac at the end of the street she saw a Ford pickup parked in front of Isabel's house, a truck with lots of hard miles on it, a bed full of holes, a body full of dents and dings. It had once been white but was now layered with brown dust. Claire was debating whether to turn around in the cul-de-sac or to stop when she saw Chuy Santos in the yard hunched over and yanking out weeds in the yard. It was hard labor in New Mexico in June when the earth was as fixed as concrete and unwilling to let go of its scrawny progeny. Weeding came easier after a hard rain.

As Claire parked, Chuy heard the gravel crunch and looked up rearranging his expression once he saw who it was.

"Hey," he called.

"Hello," she said, climbing out of her truck. The black dog that had been sitting on the ground watching Chuy work stood up and wagged its tail.

"How's it going?" Chuy asked.

"I'm all right. How are you?"

"Been better," he said. "Been a whole lot better." He seemed to be shaking something off his back as he walked over to Claire. "There's nothin' I can do for my sister now except clean up the place and pull out the weeds. We had the funeral in Our Lady of Sorrows. I wanted to scatter the ashes here or in the river, but Manuel says we're Catholics even though he's the only one who goes to church so the body has to be buried in the cemetery."

"You have my deepest sympathy," Claire said.

"*Descance en paz*," Chuy said.

"Do you live here?" she asked.

"No. I live down the road. Isabel lived here by herself and that son of a bitch Atencio knew that."

"Has the document been found yet?"

"Nope," Chuy said.

"I've been doing some research. I came across some interesting things about your family history."

"Oh yeah? Like what?"

"I told Isabel that the paper she found under the floor could have been written by a Jewish mystic in Mexico City named Joaquín Rodriguez. I read about Joaquín's Inquisition and learned that it was witnessed by an official named Manuel Santos."

"*A la.*" Chuy slapped his forehead. "You're saying our illustrious ancestor who came here with Don Juan de Oñate and the person my brother was named after was an Inquisitor?"

"It's possible," said Claire, the careful archivist, wondering how she would feel if she heard similar news about her own ancestor.

Chuy surprised her with a laugh that was short and sharp

as a bark. "We've been called many things, but an Inquisitor? That's a new one. It would piss my brother off to hear that, but me? I wouldn't give a shit if it was true. Hell, my given name is Jesus and our last name means saints, but in spite of our name none of us are descended from saints. We're all mutts like Blackie here. Scratch a New Mexican and you find Spanish blood, Moorish blood, Inquisitor blood, infidel blood, Marrano blood, Indian blood and who the hell knows what other kind of blood? Maybe even some white dude's blood." He laughed. "Four hundred years in this state and people are still worryin' if they have *limpieza de sangre*. We all bleed red, but none of our blood is pure. Every one of us has dirt on our hands." He looked down at his own hands covered with yard dirt. Then he rubbed his nose and transferred some of it to his face. "I'm ready for a cold one," he said. "And you?"

"All right," Claire replied. She didn't want a beer, but she hoped to keep Chuy talking. She sat down at the picnic table and the dog followed. She patted his head while she waited. The phrase "we all bleed red" was familiar. She tried to place it and concluded she had come across it in a novel she'd read recently about Albuquerque gangs. By the time Chuy returned with the Coors Lite, the dog's head had settled in Claire's lap.

"Negrito," he said. "Get your goddamn nose out of there." He gave the dog a shove. The dog moved away but with a wag of its tail indicating it intended to come back.

Claire took a sip of the beer. "Do you know if Tony Atencio was a gang member?" she asked.

Chuy shrugged. "I don't know for sure that he was in a gang, but he's a gangster."

"Do you think he is capable of killing Isabel?"

"Sure, why not? Who else could have done it?"

"If the document is what I think it is, it could be very valuable."

"Who knew about it," Chuy asked, "but you and May Brennan? Isabel didn't tell me."

"Did she tell Manuel?"

"Not that I know of."

"It's possible Isabel consulted someone else. May gave her the names of two experts in the field."

"Possible," Chuy said, sipping at his beer.

"What do you do?" Claire asked.

"Me? I've done a lot of things. I was earning my living at the Santa Ana Casino until they cut me off." He laughed. "Gambling for a living isn't very secure, but hey, when is life ever secure? Two bodies in our house in one week. First Isabel and then the skeleton under the floor. Now I learn that our ancestor could be an Inquisitor. Are those OMI dudes gonna be able to tell us that?"

"Lieutenant Kearns said the skeleton was a man."

"Why didn't he tell me? The bones were found in our house." Chuy guzzled the beer and put the can down. It thumped the table with a gimme-a-refill sound.

"I'm sure he'll tell you. He just happened to see me first."

"How do they know it was a man?"

"Men have more slope to their forehead."

"Just like the monkeys, right?" Chuy stood up. "How about another beer?"

It was late in the day. Darkness approached and cast its shadows before it. Dusk was quiet at this time of year before the cicadas started their evening shrill. Claire stood up, too, putting down her nearly full beer. "I should go," she said.

"Stop by any time," Chuy said. He kept up the wise guy

banter, but his shoulders sagged when he stood as if he was carrying the weight of his sister's death. When Claire looked in his eyes she saw the brown bleeding into the white.

She took the back way home through Sandia Pueblo. When the pueblos allowed development at all it nibbled at the edges of their land near population centers. There was no development on Sandia land between Bernalillo and Albuquerque, only fields where cattle grazed, a cottonwood bosque on the west and the Sandias on the east. The sun had moved behind the West Mesa, taking with it the dazzling light and leaving behind a more subtle landscape. It was the hour when the mountains seemed to want to speak. Claire thought if she could only listen carefully enough she would hear. The shadows created a backdrop and the space allowed room for her imagination to wander. It took her far away from fingerprints and VCR's.

She checked her E-mail when she got home and found offers to consolidate her debts and to connect her with hot college studs but nothing from Pietro Antonelli.

chapter ten

 On Sunday she woke when daylight came through her bedroom window. Skipping her morning tai chi she let Nemesis out, followed him into the yard and tended her roses. Gardening was a form of meditation and the best time to practice was early in the morning when there was still a lick of coolness in the air. During the night the temperature dropped thirty degrees in the desert but the heat returned as soon as the sun crawled over the mountain. Claire's house was in the foothills of the Sandias and still in deep shadow. She watered the roses and dead-headed the spent blossoms enjoying the coolness left over from the night. The Don Juans were a deep, dark red, the color of love, the color of blood. The dead petals fell to the ground and spun away in a gust of wind.

She hated the thought that Isabel Santos was dead. She would hate it even more if the death had been caused by anything as trivial as a VCR. She knew that most murders were impulsive, provoked by alcohol and/or anger. A former Albuquerque policewoman told her the police were thrilled if they came across a crime scene where the murderer had given it more than five minutes thought; they liked to occasionally be given a challenge. As she nipped off the roses, Claire considered whether she had selfish reasons for hoping the cause of Isabel's death was not the interruption of a petty robbery. She had a mother's response of not wanting to see a young person die and a thinking person's response of hating to see death be meaningless. There was also the issue of guilt. She had no reason to feel guilt if the thief had been after a VCR. She needed to feel guilt only if the thief had gone to Isabel's house looking for the last words of a mystic named Joaquín. That death could have been prevented by bringing the document into the secure shelter of the center.

The sun had come over the mountain and burned the coolness from her skin, but dark of the night emotions lingered. She remembered the words "Everything is upside down. The garrote or the fire. Give me the fire. Adonay is my God." She knew Isabel had not made up those words. Claire was convinced there had been an important document under the floor of Isabel's house. Either it had been destroyed or the person who possessed it now had not come forward. Tony Atencio had provided the police with little incentive to look further. They needed evidence to motivate them. Claire wondered where that evidence would be found. She went inside, made herself a cup of coffee and called August Stevenson.

"And how are you this fine morning?" he asked.

"I'm struggling with the death of Isabel Santos," she replied.

"I'm sure you are."

"I talked to May Brennan and Lieutenant Kearns yesterday. The boy they have in custody is a strong suspect, but the police haven't charged him with murder yet. May said she gave Isabel the names of Warren Isles and Peter Beck, but there's no evidence she contacted either one of them. Can you tell me anything about these men?"

"I know Peter Beck by reputation only."

"And what is that?"

"That he knows more about the Mexican Inquisition than anyone else in this country. Warren Isles lives in Santa Fe. I hear he has deep pockets and has been buying up documents related to New Mexico history. John Harlan could tell you more about that."

"How did he come into his money?"

"Selling mutual funds. Have you ever noticed how people with boring jobs turn to history? New Mexico history will relieve boredom like that of no other state."

"It has been lately," Claire said. "If someone offered the document to Isles without revealing its source, do you think he would buy it?"

"It's possible," August replied. "I would consider that unethical myself, but ethics may not be an issue with Warren Isles." Before he bid her good-bye he gave her a warning. "If you're thinking that someone killed Isabel Santos over a document related to the Inquisition, you ought to consider what that person would do to you. The Inquisition is a grim subject. Anyone who spends too much time thinking about it is likely to have a dark side. My advice would be to turn the names over to the detective and go back to your regular job."

Sleuthing had become her regular job, Claire thought, but she thanked August for the advice and hung up the phone.

On Monday she checked her messages and mail at the center then went to Celia's office and found her adding a bottle cap magnet to her Frida Kahlo shrine. Frida Kahlo was a Mexican artist who had a short, painful, but brilliantly creative life. She painted her way out of a horrible accident and a difficult marriage to the philandering Diego Rivera.

"Another tribute to Frida?" Claire asked her.

"Yes," said Celia, who today was wearing a gray linen dress and a necklace made of silver elephants.

There was a portrait of Frida Kahlo inside the bottle cap. Even in this scale her eyebrows looked like ravens in flight. Claire considered the clothes and the shrine to be a form of rebellion against the restrictions of academia. Celia was very good at her job and she had tenure. She couldn't be fired, but she could be pushed aside, given an office in the basement and nothing to do if someone like Harrison Hough took a dislike to her. Playing up her ethnicity could be an insurance policy. Even Harrison wouldn't dare create the appearance of getting rid of a woman for being too ethnic.

Celia found the perfect spot for the bottle cap then turned to Claire and said, "What's up?"

Claire told her about the visit to May Brennan. "What do you know about Warren Isles and Peter Beck?" she asked.

"I've seen Warren at historical conferences but I never met him. He's a doughboy with soft, white, greedy hands. If the document is ever found, he'd be a good person to buy it and donate it to the center, if he could be talked out of keeping it for himself. His name on a plaque in the library might give him an incentive."

"And Peter Beck?"

"His scholarship is impeccable. As a person, he's a prick, but that goes with the territory, doesn't it? The bigger scholars get, the more arrogant they become. He knows everything there is to know about the Inquisition in the New World, but he's so pedantic he manages to make even evil and cruelty boring. His book is duller than dust. Speaking of pedants, you haven't said anything about this to Harrison yet, have you?"

"No."

"Don't."

"May also told me that the first person in the Santos family to settle in Bernalillo was named Manuel and he came north with Oñate. Manuel Santos is also the name of an Inquisitor who witnessed the execution of Joaquín Rodriguez. I came across that in a document August sent me."

"I suppose it's possible Manuel Santos, the Inquisitor, or a relative came north with Oñate, but you'd have to wonder what would motivate a family in a position of power in Mexico City to leave it for the wilderness of el norte."

Claire went back to her own office with no warning from Celia to be wary of Inquisition experts or anyone else. It wasn't Celia's nature to be careful.

chapter eleven

When Claire left work she usually went out the back door to the parking lot behind the library, but tonight she planned to attend a reading at the bookstore so she left by the main door and walked across Smith Plaza. It was evening, there was a light breeze and shadows danced on the wind. The man walking across the Plaza had something rarely seen in Albuquerque-style. His well fitting suit made him seem out of place. Suits were seen occasionally at UNM, but they rarely had style. Suits at UNM bagged at the elbows and the knees. The man had a self possession that made the near-empty plaza seem like a stage for his solitary walk. He was slim. He held his head high. He had black, wavy hair. Many would consider him good-looking, but the quality Claire noticed most was his focus. His name was Manuel Santos.

"Can we talk?" he asked when their paths met in the middle of the plaza.

"All right," she replied.

They stood still for a minute considering where to go. Manuel was Claire's height although he had appeared taller at a distance. Since this was her territory it was up to her to name a suitable place. She was done with her office for the day. It was too nice to go back inside. She suggested they sit by the duck pond and they walked to a bench that overlooked the water. Manuel sat down, leaned against the corner of the bench and draped his arm across the back. It settled into the curves of the wood as naturally as a snake nestling on the branch of a tree.

"Chuy told me you came to the house," he began.

"I did."

"What is this talk about us being descended from an Inquisitor?"

"I did some research into the document Isabel found and came across a record of Joaquín Rodriguez's Inquisition in 1596. One of the officials who witnessed the event was named Manuel Santos. According to May Brennan, a Manuel Santos came north with Oñate's expedition and was one of the first settlers in Bernalillo. Did you know your family was descended from a settler who was part of Oñate's expedition?"

"Of course," Manuel said. "But I never heard that our ancestor was an Inquisitor. Do you have any proof that the name isn't just a coincidence?"

"No, but if the document Isabel found was written by Joaquín Rodriguez, it would establish a link between the two men."

"There is no proof there ever was a document. There is only your word." He looked like a lawyer today and now he began to sound like one.

"Of course there's proof," Claire said. "There's the note in Isabel's handwriting. The authenticity of her handwriting is easy enough to establish."

"I'm not denying that, but the note you produced was not

signed Joaquín Rodriguez or Joaquín anyone else. It wasn't signed at all."

"Isabel told me it was signed Joaquín."

Manuel didn't need to say the words "hearsay, inadmissible"; his hard amber eyes said it for him. They were Isabel's eyes in shape and in color, but not in warmth of expression. "For all we know Isabel wrote that note in your office and those were words you asked her to write."

He remained cool in his lawyer's suit but Claire began to sweat in her summer dress. She hoped her face wasn't flushing to reveal her anger. "That's not true," she said.

"We found no notebook with lined pages in the house."

"The police found the cross. There was a skeleton beneath the floor."

"They found nothing inside the cross. It's not so unusual for an old house to have a skeleton buried underneath it."

"If the skeleton belongs to a member of your family that could be established by DNA testing."

"Yes, but that would require samples of current DNA for comparison. Why would I want to subject myself and my family to that?"

"Because you care about what happened to your sister and you want to know the truth."

Manuel's eyes demonstrated how hard lawyers could be while his hand tightened around the railing on the back of the bench. "I know the truth. My sister walked in on Tony Atencio while he was robbing our house and he pushed her. She fell, hit her neck against the table, ruptured an artery and it killed her. It's brutal. It's stupid. But that's the way crime is."

Was this the truth of his sister's death? Claire wondered. Or the spin a politician chose to give it?

"You would be doing my family and Isabel a service if you

dropped all this business about Inquisitors and Jews."

"The document Isabel described could have enormous historical significance. Don't you care about finding it?"

"For me and my family seeing that Tony Atencio pays for his crime is a priority. Finding the document is not."

Before Claire was able to reply, a backpack-toting student approached them. For a split second it occurred to her that backpacks could be considered a weapon and that she and Manuel might be in danger, but then the student smiled and said, "Excuse me, but are you Manuel Santos?"

"Yes?" Manuel replied.

The student extended his hand. He had the short blond hair and earnest manner of a Mormon missionary. "I'm Charlie Bowles, president of the Young Republicans Club on campus. It's such an honor to meet you."

"My pleasure." Manuel smiled a professional smile and shook the student's hand.

Claire had been wondering whether Manuel Santos the slick politician would surface. She wasn't surprised he could turn on the charm when he wanted to, but the quickness and completeness of the change were as startling as a lightning flash.

"Would you be willing to speak to our group some time?" the student asked.

"Of course," Manuel said. He handed a business card to him.

"Thank you," the student gushed, taking the card and walking away.

It took longer for Manuel to turn off the charm than it had taken to turn it on. Still basking in the glow, he turned toward Claire. "Are we done?"

"Yes," Claire said.

"My family will be suffering from the death of my sister for a long, long time. We would be grateful if you would let us deal with our grief in our own way."

She remained seated on the bench while Manuel walked across the plaza accompanied by his shadow. Smith Plaza wasn't that large, but it was bordered by the massive library building. When it was empty it reminded Claire of public spaces in Mexico, the plazas where the Aztecs ripped the still-beating hearts from their prisoners, the Spanish slaughtered the Aztecs, the Inquisitors tied Jews to the stake and burned them to cinder. There had been plenty of violence in New Mexico, too, but there was no record of it ever being the public spectacle it had been in Old Mexico. She wondered about the effect of Isabel's murder on Manuel Santos's career. To Claire it was a dark stain that could widen and spread like ink on a blotter, but a random murder by a petty criminal might have familiar reverberations and evoke sympathy in voters. It was the kind of violence that could—and all too often did—happen to anyone. A murder related to hidden documents and family secrets would be harder to understand and explain.

When Manuel had reached the far side of the Plaza, climbed the stairs and disappeared from view, she went back to her office. She still intended to go to the signing at the bookstore, but there was something she needed to do first. She skimmed through the addresses on her computer to see who she knew at the Smithsonian. Over the years her career had created a web of contacts. She came across the names of several people she knew, but the one she knew best was Sarah Jamieson who had once been an anthropologist at the University of Arizona. The Smithsonian offered her a good job and she had reluctantly left the dry heat of the desert for the steamy heat of Washington, D.C. It was two hours later in Washington and Sarah might be home from work.

Claire dialed the number. When the answering machine came on, she said "Sarah, this is Claire Reynier, I was wondering if . . ."

"Hello."

"Sarah?"

"Claire. How have you been? It has been years, hasn't it?"

"Years," Claire said. "How are you doing? Are you liking the Smithsonian and Washington?"

"Pretty much, but I miss the desert. It gets in your blood. I hear you're at UNM now."

It wasn't exactly the Smithsonian, but Claire liked it. She told Sarah about Isabel Santos, the cross, the document and the skeleton found under the house. "It would be incredible," she said, "if that skeleton could be traced and connected somehow to Isabel's death."

"Bones don't lie," Sarah said, "and neither does DNA."

"Do you know any of the forensic anthropologists at the Smithsonian?"

"I know Harold Marcus. He's the best."

"The Sandoval County Police told me that the Smithsonian only gets involved in exceptional cases and ones having to do with paleoindian artifacts, but my impression is they don't want them to get involved. The OMI here is territorial. The Smithsonian has better resources and has a better chance of finding out what happened than anyone else. If they got interested in the case, how could local law enforcement say no?"

"Would you like me to mention it to Harold?"

"Yes, but . . ." Claire feared she was exceeding her authority.

"I won't say you're suggesting the Smithsonian get involved, only that you told me about a very interesting case." Sarah had an intuitive understanding of people and was good at management. Claire was not. Claire had never learned how to persuade other people to do her bidding. "Thanks," she said.

The conversation moved on to work, old friends and ex-husbands, ending in a promise to get together soon. It was a sincere promise, but they both knew it was unlikely to happen unless something brought one to the other's city.

As Claire hung up the phone she had the sensation that she wasn't the only person working late at CSWR, that someone had been wandering through the corridors.

"Hello," she called, but there was no answer. She gathered up her belongings and left her office. As she locked the door behind her, she heard the gate that led from the library to the center creak open and shut. When she went through the door and entered the library herself, she found the great hall empty.

It was still light as she walked across campus. Usually the bookstore closed at six, but this was a special event honoring a well-known woman writer from South America. She gave a passionate reading that went on longer than Claire expected. She waited in line afterwards for a signed first edition.

When she left the bookstore night had fallen. Except for an occasional megaphone of artificial light suspended beneath a street lamp, the campus was dark. As she passed by the construction site that had once been the Student Union, she became aware that she was very much alone. She enjoyed that rare sensation during the day, but it wasn't so pleasant at night. Student escorts were available after dark, but she never would have called one. This was where she worked and spent much of her time. In a way it was her home.

As she headed toward the steps that led down to Smith Plaza she heard footsteps behind her that seemed to echo her own. When she took a step, the echo took a step. She didn't want to turn around and give the impression that she had noticed or was afraid. She continued walking. The footsteps continued following. When she reached the steps she took a diagonal path, turned her head slightly and glimpsed a man in the glow of a light. She turned back toward the library and began descending the steps at a rapid pace. The man was still walking on level ground. Their footsteps got out of sync, but it sounded as if he, too, had picked up his pace. It became a syncopated beat rather than a literal echo. At any time someone could have come out of the library or the Humanities Building, but no one did. Claire and the man remained the only people within sound or sight.

She began to cross the open space of the plaza where there was no cover. In a sense the openness provided protection. Whatever happened here could be seen from the library, if anyone was watching. Still she kept on walking as fast as she could without appearing to be running away.

The footsteps stopped and once again the only sound she heard was the beat of her own feet. The lights from inside Zimmerman Library spread across the steps and beckoned.

She crossed the plaza, climbed up the stairs to the library and let herself in through the glass doors. Zimmerman wasn't buzzing with activity at this hour, but it was in operation. Students manned the information desks. A guard sat on the bench. She looked through the door that faced the plaza and saw no one. The man had stepped back into the shadows or had turned and walked away.

She could have asked the guard to escort her to her truck in the back lot, but to ask for help would mean admitting that she thought she'd been followed and she wasn't ready to do that. Besides, the guard appeared to be half asleep. She walked around the corner to the ladies' room, took her key chain from her purse and inserted the keys between her fingers with the sharp ends protruding. She walked out the back door toward the parking lot with her keys at the ready but no need to use them. No one was on the walk, no one was in the lot. She got in her truck and drove home.

chapter twelve

After work the next day she went to see her friend John Harlan who was an antiquarian bookseller at Page One, Too. Their friendship dated back years to the time when they were both married. John had become a widower. Claire had gotten divorced. There was a possibility that they would become a couple after they both became single, but it hadn't happened yet. John was seeing another woman. Claire was waiting for a message from Pietro, which resembled waiting for a message in a bottle. She thought about him as she drove through the traffic to Page One, Too. What was she expecting to hear anyway? The chances were overwhelming that Pietro was married. In her more detached moments she wondered if she day-dreamed about him because he was in some ways a known quantity, or was it because he lived in Italy and was most likely unavailable? They had parted many years ago with regret but no bitterness on her part. It was safer to contemplate reuniting with a long distance lover she had once known than moving forward with a person who, as a lover anyway, was unknown.

"Hey, Claire," John said when she entered his office, which, as usual, was piled high with books and papers. He stood up, brushing his hand across the top of his head, giving it an electrical charge. "How's it going?"

"I'm good. And you?"

"Not too shabby."

"How's Sandra?"

"Fine," he said.

Claire thought she would prefer a little more enthusiasm if she were Sandra.

"Have a seat. What's on your mind?" he asked, sitting down himself and preparing to play the role of book dealer psychologist. Claire knew that psychology often came into play when buying and selling books, particularly when coaxing people to part with their books.

"How do you know anything is on my mind?"

"You look worried."

"I do?"

"Yup."

"Tell me what you know about Warren Isles."

"He's a good customer. He's interested in New Mexico history. He's got a lot of money."

"How did he get his money?"

"By coaxin' old ladies to part with theirs, persuading them to invest in mutual funds during the boom years of the nineties. Trust me." He laughed. "Getting old ladies to part with their money is not as easy as you might think." He leaned back in his chair. "What is your interest in Warren Isles?"

"Strictly professional," she said. "Have you heard about the murder of Isabel Santos, a young woman who lived in Bernalillo?"

"There are a lot of murders in New Mexico," John said.

"What's special about this one?"

She told him the story of Isabel Santos and the document she found.

"You think the document was stolen from her?"

"It might have been."

"What good would that do a thief? It would be like having a stolen Van Gogh. You'd have to keep it in the closet; you'd never be able to show it to anybody. That would take all the fun out of owning it, wouldn't it?"

"May Brennan gave Warren's name and number to Isabel. Is this a document he would want to add to his collection?" she asked.

"It's possible. He's been buying up a lot of stuff related to New Mexico history and paying a good price for it. He's especially interested in the Penitentes."

"Would this be considered New Mexico history or Old Mexico history?"

"I'd say both if it was found in New Mexico. You're sure that the document Isabel found was written by a Jew?"

"Yes."

"You know the Penitentes were—and still are—very secretive. It's a tight brotherhood that flourished in remote New Mexico villages. They meet in their *moradas*, their places of worship. They say their prayers, they conduct their rituals, they reenact the crucifixion. The church frowned on their practices. The Jews had to be secretive about their practices, too. Both groups were outside the control of the church. They lived in areas where the padres seldom visited. Some of the ephemera I sold Warren speculates that the Penitentes allowed the Jews to worship in their *moradas*. No one except for those involved will ever know if that is true or not. It may be interesting to speculate, but you're never going to find out the truth about a people who practiced their religion in secret for centuries."

"I didn't realize you knew so much about the subject," Claire said.

"If you want to become an expert on a subject quickly, this is a good one. It is so shrouded in secrecy you can claim anything you want to claim. Who's to deny it?"

"Peter Beck? He's the leading scholar of the Mexican Inquisition."

"Now there's a fun job. Can you imagine spending your working hours thinking about all the innocent people the Inquisition slaughtered in the name of God? Would you want anything to do with that God?"

"I have very little to do with Him," Claire confided. "But the concept of a masculine God still exists in my psyche. I don't know why I do it, but when I'm worried or in trouble I find myself consulting with Him and bargaining with Him."

"Conditioning," John said. "In Texas where I grew up we were raised in the Baptist tradition of a masculine God. It's hard to break away from that. It probably wasn't all that different in Tucson. You were raised an Episcopalian, right?"

"Right."

"When you're a Protestant the differences between the denominations seem large, but once you break away, they all look pretty much the same. Catholics are another story. People don't break away. Once that church gets a hold of a person it doesn't let go. They still have a tight grip in New Mexico."

Claire never knew where a conversation would go when she visited John. The piles of books and papers and the clutter in his office made it a comfortable place to sit and chat.

She also never knew when a conversation would be interrupted. A customer appeared at the door and ended this particular conversation.

"Nice talkin' to you," he said to Claire, standing up to greet the customer.

"You, too," she replied.

Checking the E-mail when she got home had become as routine as letting the cat out. That night she checked it again to find an extensive selection of credit card offers. She made herself a salad and was sitting down to eat it when the phone rang. She checked the caller ID box and saw anonymous, one step up from unavailable. Occasionally anonymous was a real person instead of a computerized phone dialer that reached 500,000 people a day. On a whim she answered. The line was full of the static caused by distance and time.

"Hello? Is this Claire?"

"Yes."

"This is Pietro. Your old . . . friend, Pietro Antonelli." She knew that the minute she heard his voice.

"Pietro. It's so good to hear from you. How are you?"

"I'm fine. And you?"

"Fine."

"It was such a wonderful surprise to get your E-mail. You are living in New Mexico now and working at the University library?"

"Yes."

"I teach American literature at the University of Florence. It was so amazing to hear from you after all this time. I've thought about you often and wondered how you were."

He had taken the step of calling her. Now she had to plunge into cold water to find out what his marital status was. "I got divorced a few years ago and started a new life. I'm doing well now. I have two grown children. My daughter Robin is in graduate school at Harvard. My son Eric is in the computer business in Silicon Valley in California. Do you have any children?"

"I have a daughter Sophia who is sixteen. She is very beautiful."

"I'm sure she is." Did his daughter have his brown eyes? she wondered. "And your . . . wife . . . ?"

"My wife . . ." His voice seemed to come from an island of sorrow, someplace in the middle of the Mediterranean where the tree limbs remained bare and women in black wailed a constant lament. "My wife has cancer. It has been difficult. That's why I didn't answer you sooner. I couldn't put it in an E-mail."

"I'm sorry, Pietro. It must be awful."

"It's hard to talk about."

"What kind of cancer?"

"Of the breast." Pietro sighed into the line and changed the subject. "Tell me about your work. You said you were doing something involving the Iberian Peninsula. Something that reminded you of the time we spent together. It was a very special time."

"It was," Claire agreed. She noticed how fluent his English had become. Pietro's English had been a rather charming struggle when she knew him. "Your English is excellent now."

"I teach American literature. I had to become absolutely perfect."

"Do you remember the day we spent at the Alhambra? The time we spent looking for the Jewish quarter in Barcelona?" The souk in Rabat? The snake charmers in Marrakech? The blue doors in Essouara?

"I remember it well. You were so beautiful then, Clara."

He was the only man who had ever called Claire beautiful. The best she ever got from her ex-husband was "nice dress" or "did you get a haircut?" Even the name Clara which sounded clunky in English sounded melodic in Pietro's voice.

"Thank you."

"It's true."

"I came across a document that appears to have been written by a converso who came to the New World and was killed by the Inquisition in Mexico City. It was found buried under an old house here. It got me thinking about old Spain. To me the Alhambra is a symbol of the time when Jews and Muslims and Christians lived in harmony. Why are those periods so rare in Europe?" She didn't expect Pietro to be an expert on the subject, but she was interested in his point of view.

"There are too many people grasping for their piece of pie in Europe and the Middle East. Too much remembered hatred. Too many old grudges. The religions of Abraham are like siblings who never stop squabbling. When anything bad happens people revert to tribal warfare. They mask it in religion, but it's tribal warfare. That has always been the promise of America, a wide–open country that could absorb the overflow. I like America. I've been there several times since I last saw you."

"Really?"

"Yes. I go to academic conferences, mostly on the east coast. I've never been to the Southwest."

"There's still plenty of wide open space here."

"Someday, I hope. Well I must go, Clara. It was wonderful to hear from you. I will E-mail you my address in Florence. If you ever come to Italy you must visit. If I can help you with your research, please let me know."

"I will."

"Ciao, Clara."

"Ciao, Pietro."

After she put down the phone she wasn't hungry any more. She dumped her salad down the disposal, went outside and walked along the rose wall. When she reached the dark red Don Juans she got lost in her thoughts about Pietro. How perfect his English had become. How sad he sounded. How awful that his wife had cancer.

Claire took a pair of shears and began cutting the Don Juans until she had an armful of dark red flowers. She took them inside and arranged them in a vase thinking what a nice gift the roses would be for Pietro's family if only there were some way to get them to Italy in time to arrive red as blood and full of life.

Before she went to bed she checked her E-mail again and found Pietro had sent his home address. She clicked the return button and sent her own address. She considered adding a line saying she had some roses she wished to send but was afraid that would be inappropriate.

It was also inappropriate to be fantasizing about a former lover whose wife had cancer. When she got in bed she lay awake for a long time wondering how the youthful Pietro she had known had been marked by his wife's illness and the passage of time. No one could remain isolated forever from pain and the vicissitudes of life.

chapter thirteen

 In her profession no one could remain isolated from egotism and arrogance for long, either. She was reminded of this on Friday when Peter Beck called her at the center.

"Claire Reynier?" he asked.

"Yes?"

"Peter Beck. I'm in New Mexico to meet with Lieutenant Kearns of the Sandoval County Sheriff's Department. Your name came up in connection with the document Isabel Santos found. I'd like to get together with you. Could you meet me at Flying Star for coffee this afternoon? Say at three?"

"All right," Claire agreed. "How will I know you?" She assumed Peter Beck would be recognizable as a scholar, but he might not be the only scholar at the Flying Star.

"I'll know you," he said.

He was sitting at a table when Claire arrived. True to his word he recognized her as she walked in the door and signaled that by standing up. She waved and went to the counter to order a lemonade. When she got to the table

Peter Beck was seated and did not stand up again. Claire assumed that once was sufficient for him.

"Have we met before?" she asked, sitting down herself. If she had met Peter Beck she would have remembered; his reputation made him larger than life. He was also rather unusual looking. The outlines were unexceptional: tall, thin, with the limp, gray ponytail of a middle-aged professor who never forgot he'd been a student in the sixties. He was dressed rather elegantly for a professor in a slate blue silk shirt, but it was the face between the outlines that really distinguished him. Peter Beck had narrow eyes, high cheekbones and a prominent nose with an aristocratic hook. It was a thin, angular face except for the mouth. Beck's mouth had full, sensual lips that drooped when he wasn't speaking. It was a face that combined WASP arrogance with renegade bravado.

"I've seen you at conferences," he said. "You are an archivist?"

"Yes."

As he dropped some sugar into his espresso, his spoon clinked against the side of the cup. "You spoke to Isabel Santos?"

A waiter brought Claire a tall glass of lemonade. She thanked him and sipped it through the straw. "May Brennan gave her your name, my name, and Warren Isles's name as people who might be interested in the document she found."

"Is Warren Isles an expert on the Inquisition?"

"He collects documents relating to New Mexico history. Isabel came to my office to see me," Claire said. "She copied the Ladino words she saw on the document and gave them to me."

"What exactly were those words?"

"Didn't Lieutenant Kearns tell you?" Claire assumed Kearns would have been interested in the opinion of an Inquisition expert. Peter Beck was the foremost expert, but she didn't see any need to reinforce his ego by saying so.

"Yes, but I'd like to hear it from you."

She had no desire to try Ladino in the presence of Peter Beck so she repeated the words in English.

"What makes you think the language was Ladino?"

"The use of the words *arriva* and *abasho*."

"Couldn't that be archaic Spanish?"

"Possibly."

"And why did you think those words were written by Joaquín Rodriguez?"

"Isabel told me it was signed Joaquín." Claire felt like a graduate student presenting her thesis to a skeptical committee. No doubt Peter Beck had been on numerous committees and was skilled at turning Ph.D. candidates to quivering lumps of Jell-O. She didn't have a Ph.D. and anticipated that sooner or later Peter Beck would remind her of that fact. "Were there any other Joaquíns killed by the Inquisition?" It was a question that Peter Beck was capable of answering, but he didn't.

"Joaquín Rodriguez converted as he was led through the streets of Mexico City and he was garroted. He didn't choose the fire," he said.

"I know he was garroted. August Stevenson authenticated the documents and he gave me a copy of Joaquín's Inquisition Case."

"Ah well, that makes you an expert." Peter Beck's lips smiled slightly. His eyes remained narrow and of indeterminate color. His nose seemed to extend until it dominated his face. If he were Spanish, Claire was sure he would be speaking perfect Castilian.

He was trying to humiliate her and she was determined not to let that happen. "I'm not an expert but I am capable of reading a document," she replied. "The 'Inquisition Case' says someone in the crowd stepped forward and Joaquín spoke words that were interpreted as a conversion. Maybe that's what the Church wanted to believe. Maybe the Church staged the meeting because they were unable to convert Joaquín Rodriguez. It's possible they garroted him to save face and faked the conversion to demoralize the other Jews in Mexico. It's possible the words in the document Isabel found were his last wishes."

"That's not what happened," Peter Beck replied raising his cup to his lips and sipping deliberately. "When faced with the prospect of being burned alive, Joaquín did the reasonable thing and converted to Catholicism."

"When was Joaquín Rodriguez ever reasonable? He was a mystic who died for his beliefs, a man who circumcised himself with a pair of scissors in the Rio de los Remedios."

Peter Beck grimaced as if someone had taken the scissors to him. "Unpleasant as circumcision must have been, the pain couldn't compare to the torture of being burned alive. Joaquín Rodriguez chose to be garroted."

"Are you aware that a man named Manuel Santos witnessed Joaquín's Inquisition?"

"Manuel Santos was an official in Mexico City who witnessed numerous Inquisitions."

"Manuel Santos is the name of Isabel Santos' brother as well as her ancestor who came to New Mexico with Don Juan de Oñate."

"It's not the same person. Manuel Santos was a person of power with no incentive to leave Mexico City. He later became corregidor. His name appears on Inquisition documents well into the seventeenth century. There was obviously more than one."

"Did he have a son?"

"I've seen no record of that."

"Perhaps the skeleton will reveal more."

"You mean the one the police found under Isabel Santos's floor?"

"Yes."

"Lieutenant Kearns mentioned it. The possibility of any connection is remote."

"I'm hoping the Smithsonian will get involved; they're able to date and place skeletons with considerable accuracy."

"Why would they get involved?" Peter Beck's eyes widened enough to let in some light and show their true color. Gunmetal gray.

"It's a skeleton that could be of considerable historical significance. It could be the first Spanish settler in Bernalillo or someone who is linked to the document."

"It's more likely to be someone with no links and no historical significance. The Smithsonian is more interested in paleoindian artifacts than insignificant Spanish settlers in Bernalillo, New Mexico."

Peter's disdain made Claire even more determined to get the Smithsonian involved.

"Lieutenant Kearns asked me if I thought the document Isabel described was authentic and valuable," Beck said. "It's only fair to tell you what I told him. I'm flattered that May Brennan recommended me as an expert, but I never heard from Isabel Santos and I never saw any document. Furthermore I don't believe Joaquín Rodriguez ever wrote the words Isabel gave you. If the document existed at all, it was written by someone else and of dubious value. I pointed out that

Lieutenant Kearns didn't actually have a document, only a few lines of Isabel's handwriting on a slip of paper." Beck leaned back and waited for Claire's reaction.

"Do you think Isabel had the knowledge or ability to make those words up? She wasn't a scholar."

"Maybe she didn't. Maybe someone else did. You spoke to Isabel. You've shown a lay person's knowledge of the subject."

"You can't be suggesting that I made it up." Claire tried to hide her anger by sipping her lemonade, which was tart but not tart enough.

"You know quite a bit about Joaquín Rodriguez, a man who is far more obscure than he ought to be. You read his 'Inquisition Case'. You saw a connection between the name of a witness and the Santos family."

"I learned all that after I saw Isabel's document," Claire pointed out.

Peter Beck's cavalier shrug and supercilious smile suggested the timing of that was open to question.

"What possible motive would I have for making up such a document?" Claire asked.

"Career advancement," Beck said. "Some people advance in academia by scholarship, some do it by making attention-getting discoveries. You could call that the short track. It takes a long time and considerable effort to earn a Ph.D. It doesn't take very long to do a bit of research and manufacture a shadow of a document. Crypto Judaism is a hot topic in New Mexico these days. Everybody is coming out of the woodwork claiming to be a Marrano. Anyone who makes a discovery in that field is sure to receive attention. I passed that information on to Lieutenant Kearns, by the way."

You supercilious son of a bitch, Claire thought. She had

spent enough time in academia to have learned not to express such thoughts at the moment she had them. "That's totally ridiculous," was the only comment she allowed herself.

"Is it? Well, Lieutenant Kearns said the evidence points to a petty theft, not a document theft. Isabel apparently had the misfortune of walking in on the robbery. The Sheriff's Department has the robber in custody. Most likely that will be the end of any investigation into document theft. I hope this will be the end of your attempts to insert yourself into my field."

His eyes were full of cold contempt. He had no trouble expressing icy anger. Claire wondered if it was the only kind he was capable of expressing.

"If you will excuse me, I must be going. Pleasure to meet you, of course," he said.

"Of course," said Claire. She watched as he finished the dregs of his espresso and stood up, watched as he walked across the room. She waited until he was out the door and then she got up, too, left Flying Star and walked down the street to her truck. Only when she was inside the truck with the windows closed, the doors locked, and the air conditioner running did she grab the steering wheel and say out loud, "You supercilious, cold-hearted, mean-spirited son of a bitch."

Saying it once wasn't enough. When she got back to the center she went into Celia's office and said it again with embellishment and feeling. "Peter Beck is an arrogant, self-centered, cold-hearted, mean-spirited, supercilious son of a bitch."

"What did you expect from an Inquisition scholar?" Celia responded. "Kindness? Tolerance? Generosity?" She was wearing purple today, a rich, deep, defiant purple, the color of irises and kings.

"Intelligence," Claire said. "Doesn't intelligence imply tolerance? Is it too much to expect that from an intellectual?"

"There are different kinds of intelligence," Celia pointed out. "There is the left brain rational kind that does research, solves problems and likes to dominate. Then there is the right brain intuitive kind capable of creating art and understanding another human being. That's intelligence with compassion and heart."

"He's definitely lacking in that."

"I have a friend at Berkeley and she says Peter has been pushing the arrogance envelope there. They know even more about arrogance at Berkeley than they do here. It's the best state university in the country and they never let anyone forget it."

People pushed the arrogance envelope all the time in academia and all that ever came of it was bitching and bitterness among coworkers. It was nearly impossible to fire a person who had gained tenure.

"Why were you talking to Peter Beck?" Celia asked.

"He came to New Mexico to talk to Lieutenant Kearns and after that he wanted to talk to me."

"What about?"

"He questioned my motives and he tried to cast doubt on me and the authenticity of Isabel's document. It contradicted some of his assumptions about the Inquisition of Joaquín Rodriguez. He implied that I might have made the document up in an attempt to further my career."

"Here's another word for your list: prick."

"Thanks. I'll remember that. It would help if the original could be found."

"Are the police still looking for it?"

"They were but they might not be anymore after Peter Beck told them he doubted its existence. It would be a shame if that happens because then the original may never be found. Evidence and an important piece of history will be lost. I wondered from the beginning if Isabel could have been killed over the document. If that's true and the police stop looking for it, they'll never find the real killer. Or is this just what I want to believe?"

"It's hard to accept that Isabel was killed in a stupid robbery over a VCR."

"Is it really any different than being killed in an intelligent robbery? After you're dead, does it matter how you died?"

"It matters to the living," Celia said. "My advice is to trust your instincts and keep on looking for the document."

"Thanks," Claire said.

"*De nada.*"

Claire left Celia's office feeling grateful that she at least had never doubted the existence of the document. As she walked down the hall she felt she had left the world of Technicolor to reenter the world of black and white, the swirling world of dreams in motion for the static world of print. Celia's office was full of posters, shrines and milagros. Claire's was full of shelved books, black words on white paper. Celia acted as a thorn in the side of the somber center, although the thorn came with a rose attached. Claire saw her own role as the interpreter of other people's actions, a person who brought her own muted colors but an active imagination to the words others had written.

chapter fourteen

 On Monday Harold Marcus called from the Smithsonian. "Ms. Reynier, Sarah Jamieson told me you've come across some interesting bones. Over the years I've examined many remains, but I've never found anything in the United States connected with the crypto Jews or with the Inquisition. The combination of the skeleton and the document presents an interesting challenge. I'm an Ashkenazi Jew myself. The Sephardic Jews settled in Spain and Portugal. The Ashkenazi Jews come from Eastern Europe."

"It would be wonderful if you got involved," Claire said. The OMI forensic anthropologists were good, but they weren't the Smithsonian.

"I'm going to a conference in California this week. I could stop by Albuquerque on my way back. Would you have time to meet with me if I do?"

"Absolutely."

"I'll give the OMI's office a call and see if they could use some help."

Claire believed a call from Harold Marcus would open

the door in any but the most territorial medical investigator's office.

She had no qualms about meeting him at the center where there could be an excess of curiosity about her visitors. She still hadn't told Harrison about the murder of Isabel Santos. If anyone questioned Marcus's presence, all she needed to say was that he was with the Smithsonian. She could think of any number of reasons why she might talk to the Smithsonian having nothing to do with murder. When the student manning the information desk called, she walked out to meet Harold Marcus. He was a plump man, shorter than Claire, with rosy cheeks and a pleasant expression.

A fringe of white hair circled a bald spot on top of his head.

"Ms. Reynier," he said, taking her hand and smiling. "It's a pleasure indeed to meet you."

"Please. Call me Claire."

"That was my mother's name. To me it means clarity and light," Harold said. "I hope you can shed some light on this skeleton that came out of the darkness under Isabel Santos's floor."

"I hope *you* can."

"Let's put our heads together," Harold said.

A promising approach, thought Claire, as she led the way down the hall to her office listening to Harold wheezing behind her. She attributed the heavy breathing to the altitude of Albuquerque, the weight of Harold Marcus and/or a respiratory problem. When they reached her office, he sat down in the visitor's chair and exhaled with a sigh. She went behind her desk and sat down, too. Standing next to Harold made her feel too tall, too blonde, too WASP. She could never get away from being a WASP, but her perception of her tallness and her blondness depended on who she was with. If she and Harold were going to put their heads together in any way, she preferred to do it when they were seated and she wasn't towering over him.

"What is the altitude here?" he asked.

"A mile."

"Is that all? It feels like ten."

"Have you examined the skeleton yet?" she asked.

"First, I needed to convince the Medical Investigator, Joan Bannister, that I could be of help. Usually we get involved after they contact us."

"Did she agree?"

"Yes. We have advanced techniques for establishing the origin of a skeleton." He smiled at Claire. "So I got to look at your old bones, which appear to date from the early seventeenth century. Joan has established that the person was a young male. I examined the growth plate line on the tibia and reached the same conclusion she had: the man was in his early to mid-thirties. Even if he did live on the frontier in the early seventeenth century, that's young to die. I didn't see any broken bones or obvious signs of warfare or foul play. We'll need to do more work before we can establish the cause of death. Although the hair and nails have turned to dust, we found a few threads of fabric attached to the rib cage that I will examine further. It is entirely possible given the time and place of death that the man was an Indian. We can determine that through bone chemistry and by strontium testing of the tooth enamel. The teeth are in good shape and intact. Tooth enamel is formed in early childhood. It reflects the food and water consumed in youth and can tell us where a person grew up."

"You can tell where a person from the seventeenth century grew up just by testing tooth enamel?" Claire was incredulous.

"We can. Once the test is completed we will know whether our young man grew up in Spain, Old Mexico, New Mexico or somewhere else."

"That's amazing."

Harold smiled again. His enthusiasm for his work gave him the warm steady glow of a pilot light. Studying the dead took him into the darkness, but his intelligence transformed the experience. Claire was beginning to feel better than she had since Isabel died.

"I convinced the Medical Investigator to take me out to the site," Harold said.

"What did you find?"

"Nothing new. The investigators had dug extensively in the area around the body, but nothing else was uncovered. The fact that our young man was buried without a coffin may help to date his death or establish his ethnicity. Native Americans didn't use coffins. I'll have to do some research to establish when the settlers began using them. In the early days, they may have been too poor for wooden coffins. I understand that the settlers left in the Pueblo Revolt, but that some of them returned to their homesteads. Houses may well have been built over and over again on the same site. On the other hand, there may have been no floor or no house either when our young man was buried."

"Does your work ever deal with murder?" Claire asked.

"Of course; those tend to be the most interesting cases. Forensic anthropology has made great strides in recent years," he continued, "but sometimes we need more than forensics to make an identification. Documents and history can help." Harold's eyes were full of curiosity. "Enough about me," he laughed. "Tell me what *you've* discovered."

Claire showed him the copy of Isabel's note.

"What language is that?" he asked.

"Some say old Spanish; some say Ladino. I believe it to be Ladino."

"But you don't have the original?"

"No. The original document has vanished."

"That's unfortunate because our document people could tell a great deal from the paper and the ink. Sometimes the acidic ink on these old documents eats right through the paper and turns it to lace."

"Isabel said she found it rolled up inside a wooden cross also buried under the floor. She told me it was very old and very dry. She copied the words down because she was afraid of moving the document and damaging it. I'm afraid that it was destroyed in the robbery or that it has fallen into the wrong hands and is not being taken care of."

"I'm sure you are," Harold said with so much sympathy that Claire felt he was reaching across the desk and patting her hand. "I've read that some of the Jews imprisoned in South America in the sixteenth century wrote their thoughts down on corn cobs. One of them went to his death with those writings wrapped around his neck. Corn cobs have been known to last for many centuries in the right environment, but whether the writing on them would last I don't know. If a document was hidden inside a wooden cross and buried under a floor that would help to preserve it. We are going to examine the cross from the Santos house, date it and determine its origin.

"I've long been interested in the story of the Sephardim. My family is from Eastern Europe, but I grew up in Rhode Island. I used to go to the Touro Synagogue in Newport. It's the oldest synagogue in America, built in sixteen fifty-eight by Sephardic Jews who came to New England via the Caribbean."

"It's strange to think that a synagogue could be built in Newport at a time when Jews were being burned at the stake in Mexico City."

"They were different worlds back then, far more than a country apart. Little is known about the Inquisition in the New World. This investigation could teach us more about that dark chapter and create a wider awareness of Joaquín Rodriguez, who certainly deserves to be better known."

The dialogue with Harold reminded Claire how pleasant intellectual endeavor could be when there was a common purpose and ego was left outside the door. "I came across something interesting in my research," she said. "The Santos family is descended from a man named Manuel Santos who came north with Don Juan de Oñate. It is believed that some of the people in Oñate's expedition were crypto Jews whose names had appeared on the Inquisition lists. One of them might have brought the cross containing the last words of Joaquín Rodriguez, but Manuel Santos is also the name of a man who witnessed the execution of Joaquín Rodriguez. I have a copy of the 'Inquisition Case'. I made one for you."

"Thanks."

"I've been told that of Manuel Santos the Inquisitor, remained in Mexico and witnessed further executions."

"The skeleton could be that Manuel Santos' son."

"If he had a son. If that's the case, why were the words of a Jew hidden in the house of the family of an Inquisitor?"

"That's for us to find out. With the cooperation of the present generation it's easy enough to establish whether the skeleton belongs to a member of the Santos family."

"They're reluctant to claim an Inquisitor as an ancestor; the latest Manuel Santos is running for state senator."

"Do you know anyone else in the family?"

"I met Manuel's brother."

"Would he be willing to provide DNA for testing? Can he tell you any more about the family history?"

"I'll talk to him," Claire said.

"It's also possible that we will find no connection between the document, the cross and the bones, and that it is coincidence they ended up under the same floor. The young man who surfaced might not be related to the Santos family at all."

"I know," Claire said, feeling her optimism crawling out the open door.

"This may not have any relevance to the skeleton under the floor, but it's something I'm curious about," Harold said. "If crypto Jews came north with Oñate what was their life like?"

"I'm not an expert," Claire warned, "but I've learned that there were times during the end of the sixteenth century and the middle of the seventeenth when the Inquisition in Mexico actively persecuted Jews. However, much of the time they seemed to be ignored. They lived in remote villages the padres seldom visited. It is believed that they kept to themselves, intermarried and went on practicing their religion in secret. They continued to speak the old language. Their diet and customs were called 'the old ways'. As time passed and they went on practicing their religion in secret, some of the crypto Jews lost touch with why they were doing it."

"There's no reason to be secret anymore, is there? Why not come forward and join a local synagogue?"

"Actually there are a number of reasons. It is considered double jeopardy to be both Jewish and Hispanic. If you throw in being a woman, that makes it triple jeopardy. These are all groups that have felt oppressed at some time. By now some family members have become devout Catholics. Over the centuries the families have developed the habit of secrecy. Their Judaism is very private, very personal, not something they want to share with outsiders. The religion that they practice has its roots in the Middle Ages, and they may not feel connected to modern day Judaism."

"I've always felt that the oppression of one Jew should unite all Jews," Harold said. "Over the centuries we've faced everything from insult to annihilation."

Claire remembered the insults and stereotyping when she was in high school and wondered if Harold had found it as oppressive as she had. Jewish boys were supposed to be smart, ambitious and unathletic. WASP girls were expected to be pretty, pleasant and dumb. Young women were sought after for that reason. The dumber they acted the more popular they became. They were status symbols but it was a role she hated. It was a relief to grow older and be able to develop and express her intelligence.

"A blow against one of us should be a blow against all," Harold said.

It was the ideal, Claire thought, but it might not be the reality. Sometimes religions were as divided internally as they were threatened by external forces.

"Compared to the other religions, there are so few of us," Harold said. "There are a billion Muslims now, two billion Christians. Yet there are no more Jews in America now than there were ten years ago. Many people marry outside the religion and their children are lost. If you come across anybody in your investigations who is willing to talk about the old ways, I'd be interested in meeting with that person whether it has anything to do with the Santos investigation or not. I'm always interested in learning more about Judaism and connecting with other Jews. This is a little-known chapter back East."

"Of course," Claire said.

Harold stood up and shook Claire's hand. "It was a pleasure meeting you. Good luck with your work."

"You, too."

"I'll let you know what story the old bones have to tell."

"Thanks," Claire said.

She walked Harold out to the Information Desk.

When she got back to her office she called Chuy Santos.

She heard someone lift the receiver and pause before speaking. "Hello," a woman said in a voice that seemed rusty from lack of use.

"Hello," Claire replied. "I'm looking for Chuy Santos."

"Oh, Chuy," the woman answered. "Chuy's not here. He went to the Santa Ana Casino. To collect his paycheck, he told me."

"My name is Claire Reynier. I work at the Center for Southwest Research at UNM. Would you ask him to call me? He has my number at work, but I'll give you my home number, too."

"Of course," the woman said, taking the number down. "I will tell him to call you the minute he gets home."

CHApteR fifteen

It was hot outside when Claire left the library at five-thirty, even hotter when she got in the truck that had been baking all day in the sun, so hot she could barely touch the steering wheel. She drove across campus and was on University Boulevard before the air conditioner had cooled the cab down. Her house was stifling and full of dead air when she got home. In midsummer the days were long and full of sun. She let Nemesis out, turned on the cooler and went outdoors herself. She checked the courtyard where the datura was extending its antennae and preparing to bloom then went to her backyard to water the roses. The front of her house faced east toward the Sandia Mountains which provided a backdrop for the reflection of the setting sun and the rising of the moon, but her backyard faced the long view across the city over the Rio Grande Bosque into the vastness of the West Mesa. The weather usually came from the west and tonight thunderheads were building over Cabezon Peak. Claire couldn't remember exactly when it had rained last, but it had been months. The ground, the people, the vegetation, even the air itself held its breath longing for rain. The prickly pear and ocotillo in the foothills were parched and layered with dust. She had the sensation she had every summer that she was waiting for something she believed would come but feared might not. The sky seemed promising tonight. The clouds were darkening and the wind was picking up.

The clouds left their encampment on the West Mesa and marched across the valley preceded by a wind that reminded Claire of Pueblo feet thumping the earth and raising clouds of dust. It picked up speed as it climbed the Heights, leapt the fence and swirled into her backyard. The rose branches shimmied. There was a flash of lighting and a crack of thunder. The ambient light shifted from daylight to dusk. Nemesis ran for cover, but Claire stood still and waited on her back step for the smell, the taste, the joy of the rain. She wanted to hear it ping the roof. She wanted to see her wilted plants spring back to life. She wanted to feel rain run through her hair and down her face, washing away death, sadness, heat and dust. When the downpour started she would go inside, turn on Vivaldi's *Four Seasons* and watch the rain dance in her courtyard.

There was a crack of thunder. The wind paused from its dervish whirl for the moment of stillness and silence preceding the rain. Claire waited for the precipitation expecting the first drops to splatter the walk. It began with one drop, and then another. And then it ended. The clouds and wind passed right over the house and climbed the mountain, taking their gift to a higher elevation. In the mountains there would be a ground-soaking rain, but in the foothills it was over. Tonight had only been foreplay, reminding Claire that the monsoon promised rain many times before it delivered.

She went inside feeling she'd been let down by an indifferent lover, thinking that only the parched would pin their hopes on the weather. People on the East and West Coasts didn't sit and wait for rain. They didn't dance in the drops when it finally came. She wondered whether she had any food in her house that could compensate for the desertion of the rain, something dark and inspiring like chocolate. She rarely had chocolate in her house because whenever she had any, she ate it immediately. She found a ripe, rich mango and peeled it. *Mangos de oro*, they were called in Mexico. She remembered eating one in Guanajuato impaled on a stick like a Popsicle, the fruit carved to resemble the folded petals of a flower. She cut the mango into slices and slid them into her mouth on the tip of the knife.

She would have to water the roses now, but she put it off until morning. It was too disappointing to go back outside and see the dust on the flowers and leaves. She glanced at her answering machine and saw a blinking red light. Thinking it might be Chuy, she pushed the play button and heard John Harlan's Texas twang.

"Hey, Claire, John here. Looks like it's finally gonna rain. Damn we need it, don't we? I'm gettin' together with Warren Isles Friday and was wonderin' if you'd like to meet the guy. Give me a call."

She called him back and learned the meeting had been scheduled for the Tamaya Resort Hotel on the Santa Ana Pueblo north of Bernalillo.

"He's one of those guys who will only deal face to face and one of those Santa Feans who will only come to Albuquerque when he has to go to the airport," John said.

"But he's a good customer and Tamaya is a beautiful place. Have you been there?"

"Not yet." The resort, a cooperative effort between the Santa Ana Pueblo and the Hyatt Regency Hotel chain, had opened recently to rave reviews. Claire wanted to see it, and she hoped Warren Isles might know something about the missing document, so she agreed to meet them.

"Do you want me to pick you up?"

"I'll meet you there. I have some stops to make in Bernalillo."

"See you then," John said.

On the afternoon of the meeting the Interstate was clogged with traffic, giving Claire time to study a sky so clear and blue it gave the impression rain was a foreign language. She left I-25 at the Bernalillo exit and took Route 44 through the fast food strip, remembering the tranquility of Coronado Monument only a quarter mile away.

She passed Santa Ana Star Casino and turned at the next light eventually ending up on a one-lane road about as wide as her truck, not a road she'd want to navigate after a couple of drinks. At least it was surrounded by desert that could provide an escape route. Claire smiled at the first road sign that read speed limit 24 mph and again at the next one reading 17 mph, thinking this had the subtle, offbeat quality of Indian humor. The Santa Ana land stretched from Route 44 along the banks of the Rio Grande into the Jemez Mountains.

A magnificent stretch of Bosque was visible from the hotel. Claire passed the golf courses where water sprinklers ticked, and parked in the lot. A worker who cruised the lot in a jitney offered her a ride to the door of the sprawling building. The exterior was monumental but unexceptional. The beauty of the building became evident once Claire was inside. Every detail from the furniture, the floors, the vigas, the lights in the ceiling that resembled the skin of drums, had been carefully thought out. The artwork showed a subdued and subtle taste—Edward Curtis prints, Emmi Whitehorse paintings, photographs of Indian dancers by David Michael Kennedy, priceless Indian rugs framed and hanging on the walls. She passed through the lobby furnished like a large and elegant living room with sofas arranged around fireplaces and tables for playing board games. She entered the bar and found John Harlan nursing a Jack Daniel's.

"Welcome to my new home," he said.

Claire had been to John's home and knew it to be a dark cave of a town house bearing no resemblance whatsoever to the elegant and expansive Tamaya.

"How do you like it?" John asked.

She admired some oversized prints of horses' heads on the wall. "It's beautiful," she said.

"Warren's not here yet. Get yourself a drink and we'll sit outside."

Claire ordered a glass of Chardonnay and they took their drinks to the deck, sat down and looked across a field to the cottonwoods on the banks of the river and the jagged gray Sandias beyond. The further north Claire traveled in the Bosque, the steeper the peaks of the Sandias appeared. She liked the way the branches of the cottonwoods curved and rambled like country roads. It was a lovely place to sit, watch the light change and make small talk with John, but she didn't like to be kept waiting. When fifteen minutes had passed she got annoyed. Fifteen turned to twenty and even laid-back John glanced at his watch.

"He'll be here soon," he said. "You can count on Warren to be twenty minutes late and twenty dollars short. That's how he lets you know he's an important guy."

"Do really important people have to do that?"

"Nah, but they get in the habit and sometimes they do it anyway."

A child on the deck jumped up and down and cried out "Look."

A coyote trotted across the field. Other people on the deck stood up to ooh and aah. The coyote loped along ignoring its audience and the fuss it had created with an indifference so complete Claire found herself admiring it. Warren Isles chose that moment to show up at the table. He was a large, plump man with soft skin and a sliver of a smile that appeared to have been pasted on. Doughboy wasn't a bad description. Neither was Michelin man. Warren's skin had a rosy glow, and his hair was damp as if he had just stepped from the shower or the sauna. Had he been enjoying the spa while they waited? Claire wondered. Taken a sauna on their time?

John saw it differently. "You get stuck in traffic?" he asked.

"I never see any traffic between here and Santa Fe," Warren replied, oblivious to John's sarcastic innuendo. "Traffic picks up at Bernalillo. One reason I never go south of here unless I have to. I came down this morning, had lunch at Corn Maiden, spent the afternoon. You must be Claire Reynier." His smile curved a little higher.

"Claire, meet Warren," John said.

Warren signaled to a waiter and ordered a glass of ancient Scotch, the oldest Scotch likely to be found anywhere in the state. He sat down in the empty chair and said "Howdy" to Claire. "John told me you're interested in the history of Bernalillo."

"I became interested when Isabel Santos told me about a document she found under her floor."

"The last words of the Jewish mystic?"

"Yes."

"It was very kind of May Brennan to give her my name. I would have been quite interested, but unfortunately I never heard from Ms. Santos. Lieutenant Kearns questioned me about the document she described. I told him that given the age and the scarcity of documents in New Mexico pertaining to the crypto Jews, it could be very valuable indeed if it turns out to be authentic. I told him that no one had offered such a document to me, but if anyone did I would let him know immediately."

"I'm glad that you agree with me that the document is valuable," Claire said. "Peter Beck at Berkeley told Lieutenant Kearns that it wasn't." Claire herself wondered whom Kearns was more likely to believe. Both men seemed to be quite impressed with their own knowledge.

"I can't speak for Peter Beck, but Kearns seemed to think I was the expert in the field," Warren said with a self-satisfied glow. "I pointed out that I am not an expert in the Inquisition, but I do have one of the finest private collections of historical documents in the state of New Mexico." His aged scotch arrived and he sniffed delicately before taking a sip. "Excellent," he said.

John grinned at Claire from across the table while Warren savored his expensive scotch.

"I am very interested in the story of the crypto Jews here and collecting documents pertaining to that subject. There is nothing rarer. The subject is so secret, documentation is very hard to find. I have tried to talk to some of the old families, but they won't open up to me. If the document Isabel Santos found turns out to have a connection to New Mexico's Jews I want it."

Claire supposed that what Warren Isles wanted, Warren Isles got, but if she had knowledge about ancient and secret family traditions, the acquisitive Warren Isles was the last person she would want to share it with. She didn't trust his soft hands with their fat, greedy fingers. She didn't trust the practiced half smile used to coax valuables from women who might do better taking the long view and holding onto what they owned rather than entrusting it to Warren.

"I have the same problem with the Penitentes. They are very secretive," he said.

"John said he sold you some ephemera that implied the Penitentes allowed the Jews to practice in their moradas."

"It was an obscure article published years ago in a historical journal. John sold it to me for an outrageous price."

"Now Warren," John drawled, "you know I never sell ephemera—or anything else—for more than the market will bear."

"Right, and I am the bear market." Warren laughed at his own joke.

"Are you still in the investment business?" Claire asked.

"I've been cutting back, but I haven't retired. If you're looking to invest, I can do right by you. Women don't pay nearly as much attention to their investments as they should, often holding on when they ought to be selling."

Claire felt she gave her investments no more or no less than their due. When she inherited money she studied, analyzed, consulted, invested and forgot about it. She didn't need the money now. She didn't want to be buying, selling, trying to time the market and paying a broker a fee for every transaction. Warren Isles was the type of broker she avoided, one who took advantage of women who didn't pay as much attention to their investments as they should.

"If you're looking for investment advice, I have a very good track record."

"I'm content with my mutual funds," Claire said.

"Well, if that ever changes, call me." Warren took a card from his pocket and handed it to Claire. "Call me, too, if you should come across the original Joaquín Rodriguez document. That's something I would be very interested in."

"All right," Claire said, thinking the last place she would want to see that document end up was in Warren Isles' doughboy hands, although she was encouraged that he believed there was a document. It was more encouragement than she'd gotten from the other men she'd talked to.

John took out his briefcase to show Warren the articles and journals he had brought, the unbound material known to dealers as ephemera. Claire was reminded that she happened to be sitting at the table with a couple of dealers who had come to Tamaya to buy and sell. They began to discuss the quality and haggle over the price. John loved to deal and negotiate. His ears picked up; his eyes had the keen wariness of a coyote's.

But the negotiations soon bored Claire, and she turned her attention to the natural world, scanning the field for another glimpse of the coyote. It had vanished. The child who spotted it had gone inside with his family. The brilliant sunshine and sharp shadows were fading. She looked toward the sky and saw clouds moving in, hazy, ephemeral, wisps—not the towering thunderheads that promised rain but clouds that hung in and obscured the horizon. They had crossed the Bosque and were climbing the Sandias when Warren and John finished making their deal.

They all stood up, shook hands and left the deck. Warren now had a briefcase full of ephemera, and John's was empty. They walked through the living room and the families playing board games made Claire think of an elegant country home on a summer weekend.

"Can we walk you to your car?" John asked. "Or do you get a ride in that golf cart?"

"Neither," said Warren. "I have a dinner engagement."

They shook hands and said good-bye at the hotel door.

chapter sixteen

John walked her across the parking lot to her truck. The time of day, or the hazy weather, or the deal he'd made with Warren—something had put him in the mood for confidences.

"I'm not seeing Sandra anymore," he said to Claire as his feet crunched the gravel.

"What happened?" she asked.

"She wanted a different kind of man. Somebody who would make a lot of money and take care of her."

"Unrealistic to expect that of a book dealer."

"True." John laughed. "But I did well today. It's the Warren Isleses that keep the wheels of this business turning."

One reason that Claire stayed out of it. She felt a refreshing moisture in the air. "I was in touch with an old boyfriend of mine over the Internet," she said. "I met him in Europe when I was in college. He teaches at the University of Florence."

"Oh?" said John.

"His wife has breast cancer."

"Why did he get in touch with you?"

"He didn't. I contacted him. I didn't know about his wife."

"Spending years watching a person die of cancer is a sad and lonely business. You don't want to be disloyal, but you're ready for some love and companionship when it's all over."

Claire didn't know that Pietro's wife was dying, but she knew that John's wife had died a lingering death. "Is that what happened to you?"

"Not according to Sandra. She says I'm still thinking about my wife."

"Are you?"

"To the point where I couldn't love someone else? I don't think so, but that person isn't Sandra."

It was more open than they had ever been with each other. When they arrived at Claire's truck, she didn't know what to say until the sky took charge and left her speechless. She pointed toward the Sandias.

The sun had set beyond the golf course. The departing rays illuminated the clouds embracing the mountains and turning them into a radiant pink mist. Claire had never seen a sunset so fluid and mysterious. The Sandias were rarely shrouded in mist.

"Exquisite," John said.

There was nothing left to say. They waited for the light to fade and the clouds to turn gray again. Then they got in their respective vehicles and drove away. As she negotiated the narrow road out of Tamaya, Claire felt that the thoughts she and John had just shared had taken them ever deeper into friendship and even further away from romance. Once a man became too good a friend, once she started confiding in him about other men, it became difficult to think of him as anything but a friend, although in this case a very valuable one.

After a few miles on the Tamaya road she returned from the sublime to the commercial and was back on the strip that housed nearly every fast food restaurant known to man as well as the Santa Ana Star Casino. Wondering why Chuy Santos had never called her back and if she might find him there, she pulled into the casino parking lot and walked to the building. As soon as she opened the door she was assaulted by smoke and layers of noise. The bottom layer was background music with an unidentifiable beat and lyrics. Above that a repetitive ding, ding, ding emanated from the slot machines. That sound was punctuated by the clang of coins dropping into a metal receiver. Change? Winnings? Claire didn't know. If it was winnings, the clang should have been followed by exclamations of joy instead of more dings. There was hope in this casino, but little joy.

She walked up and down the rows of slot machines searching for Chuy. Most people played alone with a cigarette in one hand and the other on the machine. Many were older women who had little to lose. Women who were put off by Las Vegas felt welcome in New Mexico's more intimate casinos. They sucked their cigarettes and pushed the buttons like automatons. One woman appeared to be linked to her slot machine by a chain. It only took a few minutes for Claire to long for escape. If she still believed in hell, this would be it.

She gave up on the slot machines and went to the tables. A bunch of men were clustered around one table tossing dice, laughing and joking, adding human sounds to the mechanical noise. She found Chuy hunched over a green felt blackjack table while a dealer prepared to deal him a new hand.

"Hey," he said. "What are you doing here? You play?"

"I called you a few days ago and the woman who answered told me you were at the casino. You never called me back. I happened to be at Tamaya, and I stopped here on my way home."

"That was Grandma Tey you talked to. I've been staying at her house. What the hell." He signaled "no more cards" to the dealer. "I'm on a losing streak anyway. You want to go somewhere and talk?"

"Yes," said Claire.

Chuy's cell phone was on the table. He picked it up and led the way to the cafeteria with a shuffling walk. The restaurant was open to the casino and offered little relief from the smoke and noise.

"You want anything?" Chuy asked. "I'm getting a soda for my Dr. Pepper jones."

"I'd like a lemonade if you can find one."

Chuy went through the cafeteria line and came back with a lemonade and a Dr. Pepper.

"Sorry I didn't get back to you sooner," he said, lowering himself into a chair. "I've been busy."

Doing what? Claire wondered. "I thought you had stopped gambling."

"I did, but then I got lucky and I started up all over again." He put his cell phone on the table. "What was it you called me about?"

"Have you heard anything new about your sister's death?"

"Nada."

"Is Tony Atencio still in jail?"

Chuy shrugged. "Far as I know. I haven't seen him around anyway."

"I've learned a lot since I last talked to you."

"Yeah? Like what?" The light in his eyes reflected the gambler's belief in endless possibility.

"Lieutenant Kearns talked to the two experts May Brennan recommended to Isabel, and so did I. I don't know exactly what they told him, but Peter Beck, who is the leading Inquisition scholar, told me he doesn't believe that the Manuel Santos who witnessed the Inquisition of Joaquín Rodriguez is your ancestor."

Chuy slurped his Dr. Pepper. The bells in the casino continued their pounding, relentless beat. "Why not?"

"He said there was no incentive for an Inquisitor to leave Mexico at that time. This particular Inquisitor became a corregidor and was involved in other executions after your ancestor arrived in Bernalillo."

"That ought to make my brother, Manuel, happy now that he's the great brown hope of the Republican party. But our ancestor could have been Manuel Santos, the Inquisitor's son, if he had a son."

"It's possible, but that expert doesn't think so."

"Do they know how old the skeleton was when he died?"

"Early thirties I've been told."

"Who's the other expert?"

"A man named Warren Isles, a wealthy collector from Santa Fe, who buys historical documents. I just had a drink with him at Tamaya. I thought he might have heard something about Isabel's document, but he claims he hasn't."

Chuy's cell phone rang and the sound was barely audible above all the bells and whistles in the casino. It was the rare place a cell phone could ring without being annoying. "Hey, bro," Chuy said. "I can't talk to you now. I'm busy." He paused to listen. "What do you care what I'm doing? I'll have to call you later." He hung up.

"Did Lieutenant Kearns tell you that the Smithsonian has gotten involved in dating and identifying the skeleton?" Claire asked.

"Kearns don't tell me nothin' he don't have to tell me. That's cool that the Smithsonian is getting involved, isn't it?"

"I talked to Harold Marcus, a forensic anthropologist at the Smithsonian. The skeleton has been dated to the early 1600's. It might or might not be your ancestor."

"Hell, it could be an Indian. No one in my family likes to admit that we don't have *limpieza de sangre*, but why couldn't we have an Indian ancestor?"

"If you do, it's more likely be a woman." Claire knew that Spanish men were more likely to marry Indian women than the reverse.

"I guess."

"Marcus will do more tests. He told me that by testing the tooth enamel he can tell where and when the skeleton grew up."

"Is that right?" Chuy said.

"Yes." Claire was getting to the difficult part. She wished she were in a quieter place where she could concentrate and get the phrasing of her question right. "The one way to establish for sure whether or not you are related to the skeleton is by DNA testing and comparison. Would you be willing to do that?"

"I don't mind."

"Your brother said no."

Chuy laughed. "When my brother says no it means *nunca* if you know what I mean."

Claire knew.

"Maybe you ought to talk to my grandmother," Chuy said. "If she says yes Manuel might go along with it."

"Would you mind?"

"No. I don't mind. Let me give her a call." Chuy dialed a number. "Hey," he said. "It's me Chuy. I'm at the casino. I got a lady here from UNM who wants to talk to you. The same lady Isabel talked to." He listened for awhile then said. "Okay. I'll send her over. I'll be home later." He put the phone down. "She says come on over."

"It's not too late?" Claire asked. It would be convenient to stop on the way home but she didn't want to keep an elderly lady up.

"Nah," Chuy said. "She's too old to sleep. She loves to talk anytime. Here's how to get there. You go back to Isabel's house and follow the ditch road. It's the house on the other side of the field. Grandma Tey will be waiting for you."

"Thanks," Claire said.

"No problem. Now, if it's all right with you, I have to get back to work."

"Okay," Claire said. She watched Chuy shuffle back to the blackjack table and lay down his chips. She finished her lemonade and walked out through the casino.

As she pushed the outside door open, feeling she was about to be released from a noisy prison, she was greeted by the fresh smell of rain. She put out her hand and felt the touch of a gentle rain, the kind the Navajos called a female rain. Where did it come from? she wondered. The clouds she'd seen hugging the Sandias earlier had not been rain clouds. Rain was always welcome in New Mexico and she opened her arms to it. "Hello, rain," she said. If she were at home she would have stayed outside, watched it dance in her courtyard and let it wash away the sadness and the dust. She didn't want to show up at Tey Santos's house dripping wet, so she hurried back to her truck and clicked on her windshield wipers for the first time in months.

CHapter seventeen

The rain and wind picked up speed as Claire drove through Bernalillo, forcing her to turn the wipers from intermittent to medium. Isabel's death had been an undercurrent tugging at her emotions and her memory, but the minute she turned the corner onto Calle Luna it swelled into a wave. Death had a way of receding then rushing back whenever the memory of the deceased was reactivated. Claire thought of Isabel as a crushed butterfly, a bright and vibrant spirit who should never have died so young. Despair about her loss was mingled with frustration that the death seemed so pointless.

As Claire approached 625 she thought she saw a light flickering in a window. But when she reached the house, it was dark. She stopped and watched through the rain beyond the windshield wipers. Isabel's presence was strong, but Claire saw no other vehicles and no activity around the house. The windows were all dark. The light might have been a reflection of her headlights or a projection of her imagination. It was dark enough here to give her second thoughts about visiting Tey. On the other hand, people were more likely to confide and agree in the intimacy of a dark, rainy night.

She drove to the end of the street and turned onto the ditch road that passed behind Isabel's house. The road was made of dirt and was about as wide as the road into Tamaya, wide enough for one vehicle. But here she didn't have the option of escaping into the desert. On one side there was a ditch full of water, on the other a drop off into the field that surrounded the house where Isabel died. The field had been bulldozed lower than the road so when the ditch water flowed in, it wouldn't flow back out again. The road had the slickness of a surface that was about to turn to mud. The weeds stood high as a child beside the ditch. The arm of a cottonwood hung across the road, and branches full of wet leaves scraped the roof of Claire's truck.

Visibility was poor in the darkness and the rain. Claire clicked on her brights, but that only deepened and lengthened the shadows. She thought she saw a shadow lumber onto the ditch road. She blinked trying to clear her imagination. The shadow turned toward her and she faced an SUV with the headlights off and darkness as a driver. The only lights along the ditch were her headlights and the SUV seemed drawn to them like a vengeful bat. Claire felt trapped in a high-stakes gamble. The SUV gave no indication of intent to stop or turn away. Braking might stop her truck, but it wouldn't stop the oncoming vehicle. Her options were to dive into the ditch or into the field or to face a head-on collision. She was in a state of slow motion suspension, but the SUV was getting so close, she could almost hear it beating its wings.

She focused on the sounds and the feel of the dangers— the sickening impact and shattered glass of a crash or the splash and water pouring into the cab if she turned into the ditch. She swung the steering wheel toward the field. The truck lurched across the lip and stumbled into the field like a horse with a broken leg. While she struggled to regain control, it careened into a picnic table, smashing it to kindling. She swung the wheel to the left crashing into the trunk of a cottonwood. The glass on her side of the cab shattered on impact and fell to the ground. Her engine died. The headlights went out. Claire was all alone in the middle of the Santos's field with no protection. She felt around the cab searching for her cell phone. Through the broken window she saw the SUV turn onto Calle Luna with its high beams on and continue down the road.

Claire found the cell phone and punched in 911. She gave her name and location to the operator, relayed what had happened and asked if it would be possible to send Detective Romero.

"We send whoever is on duty," the operator replied.

Feeling like a stationary target inside the cab of her truck, Claire climbed out. If the SUV returned, she could disappear into the darkness on foot with the cell phone in hand. She left the truck behind, found her way to the portal of Isabel's house and stood under it listening to the rain drumming the tin roof. In the heat of the day she wouldn't have imagined that she could be so cold, so wet, so soon. She tried to see through the windows into the house, but it was darker inside than out. She shifted her weight from one foot to another searching for warmth, listening for any sound beyond the rain. She heard a rustle, a displacement of water beside the house. She heard motion, the jingle of a collar and Chuy's dog came around the corner, poked her with a cold nose and began to lick her arm.

"Are you alone?" she whispered, grabbing his collar and

holding tight, hoping the dog would provide some protection if a person came out of the darkness.

The next sound beyond the rain was the whine of a distant siren. As it got closer, she saw the lights of a Sheriff's Department vehicle flashing like a strobe.

The car parked. Leaving the headlights on, two cops stepped out.

"Over here," she called.

They turned their flashlights towards her, and she wondered if she looked as damaged as she felt.

"Are you all right?" a policewoman called. "I think so."

Claire released the dog and he ran off to greet the police. As they approached Claire became more illuminated, but they disappeared into the darkness behind their flashlights.

"That's a nasty cut you've got," the woman said.

"Where?" Claire's arm was covered in blood. "I didn't even notice."

By now the policewoman was at her side. The flashlights had turned away from Claire's eyes and she could see how petite the woman was. She took hold of Claire's arm and examined it. "It's a nasty cut but it looks like a flesh wound. I'm Deputy Anna Ortiz and this is my partner Deputy Michael Daniels."

Her partner was a burly man several inches taller than Claire with a pushy, aggressive manner. "What happened here?" he asked.

He moved in close while he questioned her, as if sniffing her breath. Drinking was an issue when someone drove off a road, but denying an accusation that hadn't been made yet would do Claire no good. She kept quiet about her glass of wine.

"I was on my way to Tey Santos's house on the ditch road when someone in an SUV pulled out of the field with no lights on and ran me off the road. I lost control of my truck when I turned and I hit the tree."

"Why were you on this road?" Daniels asked.

"This is the way Chuy Santos directed me."

"Chuy? How do you know him?"

"I knew Isabel. I came here to see her on the day she died. I've been talking to Detective Romero and Lieutenant Kearns about the case."

"Is that right?" The deputy was standing too close invading Claire's private space. "So what brought you here tonight?"

"Chuy sent me to talk to his grandmother. I thought I saw a light on in Isabel's house as I drove down Calle Luna. As far as I know her death isn't a closed case yet. Is there any possibility of getting Detective Romero to come over and look at the house?"

"I'll give him a call," Deputy Ortiz said.

While they waited for Romero, the policewoman took Claire back to the car, turned on the inside light and began filling out a report. Daniels stayed outside circling the house and property with his flashlight, looking for evidence. He came back and said, "I saw SUV tracks climbing the embankment on the south side of the house. No sign of breaking and entering."

Detective Romero approached quietly. He pulled up next to the police car, stepped from one vehicle to the other, and sat down in the back seat. He wore jeans and a T-shirt that emphasized his hard, muscular arms. His hair was cropped so short he appeared to be bald. He was younger than the police officers, but he took command with his soft-spoken manner.

"Are you all right?" he asked, examining Claire's arm. "That's a bad cut. Do you want me to take you to the emergency room or call a paramedic?"

"I'm okay," Claire said. "It doesn't hurt. I'll clean it up when I get home." The blood had clotted and caked, which stopped the bleeding. "I'm sorry to call you out at this hour."

"No problem. Tell me what happened."

He turned on his tape recorder and she repeated her story, wondering as she did whether she was giving it any change in emphasis or detail because he was the listener.

"So you think the attempt to run you off the ditch road was deliberate?" Romero asked.

"Yes. The SUV came right at me playing chicken. There would have been a head-on collision if I hadn't turned off."

"Did you see a license plate or anything else that would help to identify the vehicle?"

"It was big and black. That's all I saw. I couldn't even tell if it had a driver. There was nothing but darkness behind the wheel."

"Did anybody know that you would be driving the ditch road tonight?"

"Chuy Santos knew. He told his grandmother. I don't know whether he told anyone else."

"When did you talk to him?"

"I saw him at the Santa Ana Casino about an hour ago. He had his cell phone with him. Someone called and he said 'hey, bro'."

"Anybody could be a brother to Chuy especially when he's had a few drinks."

True, Claire thought, but he only had one blood brother. "He sounded annoyed that he'd been interrupted."

"Could you tell if Chuy had been drinking?"

"I don't think so. He didn't act drunk. He was drinking a Dr. Pepper while I talked to him." She knew Detective Romero and didn't mind raising the issue of her own drink with him. "I went to Tamaya before I met Chuy and had a glass of wine there with Warren Isles, one of the experts May Brennan recommended to Isabel. I'm sure it has worn off by now."

"One glass of wine will keep you well below the legal limit. Did you tell Warren Isles where you were going?"

"No."

"Did you see what kind of car he drove?"

"No."

"Tell me why you were going to see Tey Santos."

"I've been talking to a forensic anthropologist from the Smithsonian and he asked me to see if I could find someone in the Santos family who would allow them to do a DNA comparison to the skeleton's DNA. I thought I saw a light inside the house as I drove down Calle Luna, but when I got here, it was off. Would you be willing to go inside to see whether anyone has been there?"

"Let's do it," Detective Romero said.

They left the car and walked across the yard with the cops trailing behind. Romero stepped around the house and turned his flashlight on the truck. It was the only truck Claire had ever owned, the trusty Chevy she bought right after she split up with Evan. It was her symbol of an independent new life, and she was more attached to it than a grown woman ought to be to a truck. Seeing it smashed, made her feel that she had failed. The damage to the truck bothered her far more than the gash on her arm.

"The front end is pretty beat up," Romero said. "We need to get the vehicle towed back to the shop to investigate further. I can give you a ride home."

"Thanks," Claire said.

He had skeleton keys in hand when they reached the front door, but tried the knob before using them. The door swung open. He ordered Claire to stay outside, pulled out his weapon, stepped through the door and flipped the light switch. Deputy Daniels followed. Deputy Ortiz remained with Claire.

Romero called out "all clear" when the search was completed and Claire and Deputy Ortiz went inside. The house wasn't as chaotic as it had been earlier, but it wasn't orderly either. A rug had slid or been kicked sideways, the sofa pillows were askew, a closet door was open. Two candles on the mantelpiece had burned down, dripping wax all over their candlesticks and leaving a faint smell of smoke in the air. The mirror over the mantle was covered by a black cloth. Why? Claire wondered. So the glass wouldn't reflect what had gone on here? She stared at the covered mirror. In the depths of the black cloth, which absorbed light rather than reflecting it, she saw an image of Isabel swaying like a reed in her platform shoes. She saw the golden butterfly embroidered on her shirt. She saw someone give Isabel a hard shove, but she didn't see Tony Atencio. Was it the person in the SUV? Did Isabel have some thing or some knowledge that person wanted? She saw Isabel fall and hit her neck against the table. She saw her land on top of her purse. Claire cringed.

Romero tapped her shoulder with a light touch. "You okay?"

"Yes," Claire said. "But being in this house reminds me of Isabel."

"Her death was terrible," he agreed. "It's one of the old ways to cover the mirrors in black when a person dies as a sign of mourning."

"I didn't know that. Is Tony Atencio still in jail?" she asked.

"Yes."

"The person in the SUV couldn't have been him."

"Not him, no, but it could have been one of his homeboys."

They walked down the hallway. The mirror in the bathroom was also covered in black.

They moved on to the bedroom, which now resembled an archaeological dig. The bricks had been pulled out and stacked to the side and there was a deep hole in the middle of the room. Most of the dirt had been carted off. Romero sat on his heels and stared at the hole with his hand hovering over the dirt as if he longed to be digging in it himself but knew that was forbidden. The law that said digs were reserved for scientists wouldn't have stopped a criminal. Claire saw signs of recent activity. There was sand on top of the remaining brick floor and marks that appeared fresh inside the dig.

"Has the OMI been here recently?" she asked Romero.

"I don't know when they were here last," he said.

"Harold Marcus with the Smithsonian told me he came out here with them a few days ago."

"It might have been then."

"Do you think whoever ran me off the road was here?"

"Someone was inside the house," Romero said. "Someone lit the candles and let them burn down, but that could have happened hours ago. It could have been a family member. Let's give the officers the opportunity to examine the house and I'll take you home."

CHAPTER EIGHTEEN

They took the back road through Sandia Pueblo and didn't see another vehicle between Bernalillo and Albuquerque. The rain fell softly now and clouds scurried across the sky, indicating the storm was moving on.

"Best rain we've had all summer," Romero said. "Only rain we've had all summer."

"Usually I love the rain, but this was the wrong night to be out in it."

"Tony Atencio is still our prime suspect, but if someone did go back to the house it might open other avenues of investigation. A connection between Isabel's death, the robbery and the old bones would pretty much eliminate Tony. That's a guy more interested in scoring drugs than in history."

"He may have gone to the house after Isabel fell and taken advantage of an opportunity. That would explain the fingerprints."

"True."

"Have you found a match for the fibers?"

"No. I hear you've been doing some historical research."

"Some," Claire admitted.

"What have you found out?"

"I told Lieutenant Kearns that Manuel Santos is the name of a man who witnessed the Inquisition of Joaquín Rodriguez. But that particular Manuel Santos went on witnessing Inquisitions after someone else named Manuel Santos arrived in New Mexico in fifteen ninety-eight."

"It could be a son. The bones have been traced to the early seventeenth century by the OMI and the Smithsonian traced the cross to roughly the same period."

"I hadn't heard about the cross."

"That's the advantage of being a police officer. We get the good news first. We also get the bad news first." Romero stared straight ahead at the road. Claire couldn't see him well in the darkness but she imagined he smiled when he said that. "We can find out easily enough if those bones are Santos bones if the family agrees to DNA testing."

"It was what I intended to talk to Tey Santos about. If she doesn't agree, can you make the old bones part of the current investigation? Can you insist that the Santos family submits to DNA testing?"

"Not really," Romero said. "There's nothing to indicate the man under the floor died of unnatural causes. Even if there was a crime, it could be four hundred years old."

"Is covering the mirrors a custom everybody followed in the old days?"

"I'll ask my grandmother," Romero said.

They reached the wide turn onto Tramway and Romero took it, heading east toward Claire's house in the foothills. They passed the new Sandia Casino, an enormous building in the style Claire thought of as *nuevo pueblo grande*, a pueblo enlarged and embellished. She went to the casino once because the deck in the back was a good place to watch the full moon rise above the Sandias. She had to walk through the casino to reach the deck and was impressed by the high ceilings, the architecture, the decoration and the state-of-the-art air filtration system. It was the only casino in which she'd been able to breathe. If she was ever going to gamble, this was where she would go. But Santa Ana was expanding, too, and when it was finished it was likely to equal or outshine Sandia.

There weren't many people Claire enjoyed riding with. From what she knew of cops they were cowboys behind the wheel, but Detective Romero was a calm and steady driver. It might have been the rain, the darkness, the fact that he was behind the wheel, the threat she had faced—something in this moment made her want to confide in him. His gentleness opened doors Lieutenant Kearns's businesslike manner left closed.

She began with gambling. "The last time I saw Chuy he told me he had stopped gambling, that the casino had cut him off, but now he's back again so his debts must have been paid. He said he got lucky. What does that mean? If he wasn't gambling, he didn't get lucky in the casino. So where *did* he get the money to pay off the money he owed?"

"His brother, Manuel, has the money if that's how he wants to spend it."

Claire hoped she wasn't about to cross a line. The Santos and Romero families were native New Mexicans with similar backgrounds. She was an outsider, a woman from Arizona who lived in the foothills in a neighborhood known as the White Heights. "If it was Manuel, why would he choose to pay off Chuy's debts now?"

"Why do you think?" Romero asked.

"I'd hate to think it was to keep him quiet. A valuable

document that was in the house when Isabel died disappeared at a time when Chuy needed money."

"You think Chuy and Manuel are capable of killing their own sister?"

"I don't know. You know more about killers than I do. For me the question is more whether they would take advantage of their sister's death."

"We've talked to the experts May Brennan recommended and we haven't found any evidence that a document was offered for sale."

"If one of them bought it, would he admit it? Experts are practiced at concealing their sources. You might learn more by talking to May Brennan again."

Romero swung the car into the long, lazy curve where Tramway headed south holding tight to the wheel. "Why her?"

"May isn't as practiced at the art of deception as Peter Beck and Warren Isles. She says she didn't speak to them herself, but maybe she did." It was skirting closer than Claire liked to come to accusing an old friend of concealing the truth.

"Why would May hide the fact, if she did talk to them?"

Although Claire was sitting down, she felt like she was thinking on her feet. Thoughts about Isabel's death had been percolating for awhile but this was the first time she'd allowed these thoughts to rise to consciousness. "Because she's depressed. Because she's not thinking clearly. Because she may be on drugs or alcohol. Because she might have done something she feels guilty about. She might have revealed information that put Isabel in jeopardy. You could question her more thoroughly. You could find out what kind of a car she drives."

"I suppose you want us to find out what kind of vehicles Manuel, Chuy and Warren Isles drive, too."

"Chuy drives a beat up Ford truck. I've seen it. As for Manuel he came to see me at UNM and his manner was edgy."

"What did he want to see you about?"

"He didn't like the idea that his ancestor might have been an Inquisitor. It wouldn't be good for his career. He made it clear that he wanted me to stop looking into it."

They reached the road that led into Claire's subdivision. Romero followed her directions and turned left. The moon hanging over the mountains was draped in a black cloud. The cloud slipped off. For a second the moon was in full light before another cloud drifted over it. There were times Claire liked the complexity of a moon seen through clouds better than the black and white contrast of an unambiguous sky.

"Maybe we ought to give you a badge and let you run the investigation," Romero joked.

"I'd follow up on the document if it were up to me, but Kearns doesn't believe there was a document, does he?"

Romero searched for the right words. "He believes what the evidence supports."

"Do you think the evidence supports a document?"

"Let's say I'm open to the possibility. I'm not a person who needs to see something to believe in it."

Claire directed him to her house and he parked in front. "Do you have another vehicle you can use?" he asked.

"No."

"Are you going to be all right if I leave you here without one? It'll take a few days to examine your truck and then it will have to be repaired. I can recommend a mechanic in Bernalillo, if you like."

"Thanks," Claire said. "I'll rent a car tomorrow."

She felt a kind of current in the car. The kind caused by a man rescuing a woman from danger? Or was it that they were alone in a car at night and Claire was about to return to an empty house? She hoped her house was empty. Whoever had run her off the road had had plenty of time to come here. She thought of inviting Romero in, asking him to check the house, offering him a cup of coffee, but wondered if that would be appropriate. She liked him, his tough exterior and his gentle interior, his openness to the old ways, his respect and consideration for her. He treated her as an equal, not as an older person, or a white person, or an academic. He treated her as a woman, but not in a demeaning way. But she didn't know if she ought to be leaning on a detective at all, especially one who was at least twenty years younger than she was.

"I'll walk you to your door," he said.

"I'm okay," Claire replied.

"I'd like to check your windows and doors. Someone ran you off a road and almost killed you. There are people who knew where you were going. People who could find out where you live. We need to be sure that no one came here."

"All right," Claire agreed.

She went to the front door and inserted her key in the lock, which turned as smoothly as it always did. Nemesis, startled to see her with a man, arched his back and circled Romero warily.

"Nice house," he said.

"I like it," Claire replied.

As soon as they entered, she could see that the alarm had not been activated. She turned it off and walked through the house with Romero examining every window and every door.

He even beamed his flashlight outside. Although the ground was still wet from the rain, he found no prints.

"You're okay," he said. "No one has been here. Lock the deadbolt after I leave, make sure all the windows are locked, too, and turn on the alarm."

"Would you like a cup of coffee for the drive home?" It seemed the least she could offer under the circumstances.

"No thanks. Is there anyone you can call to come and stay with you?"

"I'll be all right," Claire said.

"Well, I need to get going." He handed her his card. "Here's my cell phone number. Call if you have any problems."

Bernalillo was so far away, Claire thought. Anything could happen by the time he got back to the Heights.

"Don't worry," he said as if she had somehow communicated her thoughts. "I'll pass the call to someone close by."

"Thanks for bringing me home."

"I'll check in with you tomorrow."

She stood in the doorway and watched him walk to his car. Then she shut the door, snapped the deadbolt into place, and walked through the house making sure every window was locked. She turned on the alarm and went into the bathroom to wash off her arm. It was caked with dried brown blood that turned red again when the water hit it. She watched the bloody water swirl down the drain remembering the deliberateness of the SUV as it headed straight for her. Was the driver trying to wipe *her* out or aiming at whoever happened to be in the way? Once the blood had washed off she could see that the edges of the cut held together and stitches wouldn't be needed. She treated it with antibiotic cream, then she got in the tub and soaked away the dirt and pain of the day resting her arm on the side of the tub so as not to wash away the cream. Nemesis was being a nudge by scratching at the door.

"Go away," she said.

He did but when she got into bed she found him curled up on her spot. She slid him gently to the far side of the bed. He could be a nuisance, but on a rainy night it was nice to climb into a warm bed. She expected that sleep would be a long time coming and she would have time to replay the events of the day, anticipating that at any minute a window would break and the alarm would sound.

She began at the end of the day and worked her way back. One positive element was that she had connected with Romero again. Kearns was in charge and to approach Romero directly was to go behind his back. But Romero's intuitive side, his connection to the community and the past, could solve this crime better than Kearns's no nonsense outsider attitude. She admitted to herself that she liked Jimmy Romero better than Kearns. Kearns seemed to see her as a pest. Romero saw her as a person. It was a comforting thought. Nemesis purred in the bed beside her. She fell asleep and didn't wake up again till morning.

Claire's first thought on waking was that a bird was singing outside her window. Her second was that her arm hurt. Her third was that something was missing. She ran her tongue around her mouth searching for a hole as if she had lost a tooth. Then she remembered her truck had been impounded by the police somewhere in Bernalillo. She was without wheels.

"Damn it," she said, jumping out of bed.

A startled Nemesis leapt out of bed behind her, landing on all fours.

Before she even brewed coffee, she got on the phone and made arrangements to have a rental car delivered. It was an expensive solution, but she had to have a vehicle. Being stuck in her house with no transportation left her feeling trapped and abandoned. Being without her truck left her feeling bereft. It was stupid to care so much about a truck, but this truck represented more than transportation—it represented a life that didn't depend on an untrustworthy husband.

Once the arrangements were completed she made herself a bowl of granola and a cup of coffee and sat down at the dining room table. The phone rang. Considerate of Jimmy Romero to call so early, she thought, picking it up.

"What happened to you last night?" Chuy Santos asked. "When I got home, my grandma told me you never showed up. Through the trees she saw all kinds of police lights at the house. The police told her you'd been in an accident."

"When I drove down the ditch road someone pulled out of the field in a black SUV and ran me off the road."

"*A la*," said Chuy. "Were you hurt?"

"I cut my arm. My truck was bashed in. I ran into a tree."

"Hey, a truck can be fixed. Be glad you're okay."

"Had anybody been to Isabel's house that you know of?"

"Not that I know of," he said, but he paused before he said it. "I need to go over there and check it out myself. Grandma still wants to talk to you. Could you come by this afternoon?"

"Is there another way to get there?"

"Sure." Chuy gave her directions by the regular roads. "I want to talk to you, too. I'll be back around three."

"See you then," Claire said.

A few minutes later Detective Romero called. "I tried you ear- lier, but I got a busy signal."

"That was Chuy Santos. He wanted to know what hap- pened last night. He heard I'd been in a wreck."

"Was everything all right last night?"

"Fine. I'm going to Bernalillo this afternoon to talk to Chuy and his grandmother."

"You got wheels?"

"Yes, a rental car is on the way."

"Lock up before you go. I'll be at the station this after- noon."

It was an unusual experience for Claire to have a man concerned about her safety, and she rather enjoyed it. Her own son, who had been putting all his energy into a start-up company in Silicon Valley, called her once a month.

chapter nineteen

Claire left at one-thirty to go to Tey Santos's house in a generic white rental car, the kind of car that could be seen in every airport parking lot. Other types of rental vehicles were available but ninety percent of the rental cars she saw resembled hers. At every stop light and turn she missed her truck. She could have been anybody in the rental car, but in her truck she was a book scout, an archivist, a person with a taste for adventure.

She wanted to drive by Isabel's house to see the damage and make sure her truck had been towed away, but she was afraid Chuy would be there cleaning up the yard and she hoped to see Tey first. She followed his directions and circled around the block on paved roads to get to Tey's, thinking this route was easier to follow than the one he'd given her, wondering why he'd sent her down the ditch.

Tey lived in a small adobe house sheltered by a sprawling cottonwood. A willow tree that was a cascade of leaves stood behind the house. A dog who could have been Blackie's sibling was lying in the yard when Claire pulled into the driveway. It wagged its tail when it saw the car but didn't bother to get up. Water from the ditch kept Tey's property green and fertile. Claire passed a well-tended vegetable garden as she walked toward the door. Between the stalks of corn, she saw tomatoes, chile, beans and squash—crops that had been growing in the Rio Grande Valley forever. One section of the garden was devoted to herbs. Claire identified mint, oregano, rosemary, sage, and the tall stalks and umbrella-shaped yellow flowers of anise. She knocked at Tey's wooden door.

"Hello?" Tey called.

"Hello. I'm Claire Reynier, the woman Chuy sent to see you."

"Okay," Tey said, opening the door.

Claire faced a tiny elderly woman wearing a faded cotton dress and leaning on a cane. Her face was as warm and wrinkled as a dried peach. Her black eyes had the alertness and curiosity of a hawk. Her nose had a prominent hook. Her white hair was pulled up in a bun on top of her head. Tendrils escaped and tumbled down to her shoulders.

"Come in," she said.

The house smelled like something baking. Claire thought she caught a whiff of marijuana but decided it had to be another herb.

"I'm so sorry about Isabel," she said. "I only met her once, but I liked her very much."

"After her mother and father died, she was a daughter to me. She had problems and went to California. I was so happy when she came back home." Tey's gnarled fingers clutched the top of her cane. "That terrible, terrible boy killed her."

"Are you sure it was Tony Atencio?"

"It was him. He's a very bad boy. Even my dog didn't like him and growled when he walked by. Sonny started barking when he heard him running down the ditch that awful day."

"Did you see or hear anything else that afternoon?" Although Tey was an old woman, she'd given no sign she was hard of hearing. Her body might be slowing down but her mind and senses seemed sharp.

"Nothing."

"Chuy said you heard about the incident last night. I was driving here along the ditch when a black SUV pulled out of the field and tried to run me off the road."

"An SUV? What is that?"

"A sport utility vehicle." Tey's expression remained confused, so Claire added "it's a cross between a car and a truck. Do you know anyone with a car like that?"

"I think Tony Atencio had one. Would you like some yerba buena tea?"

"I would. Thank you."

"And a cookie?"

"Yes." Claire sat down at a table covered with a flowered plastic tablecloth while Tey prepared the mint tea. "Yerba buena" translated literally into "good herb". "When the SUV ran me off the road into Isabel's yard I hit a tree."

"Don't worry. Those cottonwoods, they are very old and very strong like me." She smiled and her skin crinkled. "You can't hurt them."

"I called the police. That's why you saw all the lights."

"Even in the rain they were very bright."

"I thought I saw a light inside Isabel's house when I drove by. The police went inside later to investigate. The door wasn't locked."

Tey put the tea down on the table along with a plastic bear full of honey and a plate of cookies. "Why lock the door now that my sweet *nieta* is gone?"

"Could anyone else have gone inside the house?"

"Yes, but why would they? There's nothing left to steal."

"Do you go there?"

"Often. I talk to my Isabelita. For me she is still alive in that house."

"I felt that way, too," Claire admitted. "Someone left candles burning."

"I did that."

"Did you cover the mirrors in black?"

Tey nodded. Her hands resting on the table had the bulbous joints of rheumatoid arthritis. "It's the old way, *las costumas de antiguas*, something we do. It's not good to be looking in the mirror when someone dies. My mother taught me those ways. I wanted to teach Isabelita, but I didn't have the time. Have a cookie." She handed the plate to Claire.

She bit into the cookie. "These are delicious. Did you use anise from your garden?"

"Yes. It's a good plant."

"You have a beautiful garden. Has your family lived here for a long time?"

"For four hundred years," Tey said, "God has kept our garden green. The first Santos came here with Don Juan de Oñate."

It was the door Claire had hoped would open. "Did you know that there was an Inquisitor in Mexico City in fifteen ninety-six with the name of Manuel Santos?"

Tey's eyes were fierce. "That person is not my ancestor. My ancestor was not part of the Inquisition."

"You know about the skeleton that was found under the floor?"

Tey nodded, shaking loose a few more tendrils of hair.

"That man lived in the sixteenth and seventeenth

centuries. He was in his thirties when he died. He could have been Manuel Santos, the Inquisitor's son."

"No," Tey said, placing one gnarled hand over the other. "He could not."

"The medical investigators could find out if he is your ancestor by testing your family's DNA."

"DNA? What is that?"

Trying to explain DNA was daunting, so Claire settled for: "The medical investigators can take a piece of hair or skin or even saliva and compare it to the skeleton. They can tell from that if people are related, even people who lived four hundred years apart."

"The investigators can do that?"

"Yes, but they need your cooperation and your permission."

"I will have to ask my grandson. He is the one who has the Manuel Santos name." Claire felt the door had closed again; she knew what Manuel would say.

"Do you know anything about the document Isabel found or the cross?"

"Nothing," Tey said. "I never even saw them. She told you, but she didn't tell me. I will never understand that."

"Maybe she didn't have time."

"Maybe. The police have the cross now."

"Do you know who has the document?"

"No." Tey pushed herself away from the table to stand up. She went to a canister on the kitchen counter, picked out a stem, brought it back to the table and dropped it into her tea. "My arthritis is hurting me," she said. "It does that when it rains."

"What's that?" Claire asked, expecting to discover another good herb.

"Marijuana," Tey replied. "It's very good for the arthritis. I grow it myself between the corn stalks."

"Here?"

"Why not? It's my land. I was born here. I grew up here. I came back after that no-good man I married left and took the Santos name again. What are they going to do? Arrest a ninety-two-year-old woman and put me in jail with that Tony Atencio? Wait till they see what I would do to him."

Claire was reminded that people who lived to a ripe old age had a strong will. "Do you smoke the marijuana?"

"Only when the pain is very bad." The dog in the yard began to yip. "That's my grandson. That's the way Sonny barks when he hears Chuy."

"Don't get up," Claire said. "I'll let him in."

"Chuy can let himself in," his grandmother said.

Claire stood up anyway, went to the window beside the front door, and watched Chuy park his truck and walk across the yard. The dog stood up, wagged its tail and let Chuy scratch its head.

"Whose car is that, Grandma?" he asked as he pushed open the door. He was wearing his Santa Ana T-shirt and jeans that were caked with dry mud.

"Mine," Claire said.

"*Hola*, Chuy," Tey said.

"*Hola*." Chuy bent over, kissed the top of her head, then turned to Claire. "I thought you said you were coming later."

Claire could think of no excuse for her early arrival so she changed the subject. "Were you at the house?"

"Yeah."

"Was my truck there?"

"No. It was gone, but I could see the scar where you hit the tree. That must have hurt."

"I cut my arm," Claire admitted. "How did the house look?"

Chuy shrugged. "Looked the same to me. I didn't see any SUV tracks in the yard. The only tracks I saw went from the ditch to the picnic table to the tree like the truck had had too many beers."

"Have a cookie, Chuy," his grandmother said.

He took a cookie from the plate, snapped off a piece and crunched it in his mouth.

"The police saw the tracks last night," Claire told him.

"Did they?" asked Chuy. "Well, maybe it was one of Tony's homeboys who went back to check the place out."

"What kind of vehicle does your brother drive?" A lawyer living in the hills of Placitas would likely have an SUV, Claire thought.

"Manuel?" Claire saw ambivalence toward his older and more successful brother ripple across Chuy's fluid features.

His grandmother was quick to remind him that Manuel was Chuy's brother. "Your brother does not drive a black car," she said.

"Right. His SUV is gray," Chuy said. "A black car like that drove by yesterday afternoon when I was in the yard, but I couldn't see who was inside it."

Tey's sharp eyes told Chuy his statement had not gone far enough.

"My brother was home last night anyway," he added. "I called him and then I went up there after I left the casino." He looked to his grandmother for approval.

She nodded.

Claire thought that Manuel could have easily been at Isabel's house while Chuy was still at the casino, but she didn't say so. A wall of family solidarity had gone up and shut her out. She couldn't tell if this was a knee–jerk reaction to an outsider, if the Santoses had something to hide, or if they just valued their privacy.

The marijuana in Tey's tea hadn't dulled her mind. "The medical investigators want to compare our bones to the old bones to see if we are related to an Inquisitor. I said we would have to ask Manuel."

"Sure, Grandma," Chuy said, sitting down next to his grandmother and putting his hand on top of hers. "If that's what you want."

Claire saw this as a signal that it was time for her to go. She thanked Tey for the cookie and tea and said good-bye.

In her white rental car she drove out of the yard. In a way the car was cover, but the cover had been blown now that Chuy had seen it. She couldn't drive by Isabel's house anymore without feeling that she would be noticed. She had been wanting to visit Isabel's grave and this seemed like a good time. Tey and Chuy were occupied; she wouldn't have to worry about running into them at the cemetery. She'd be free to think her own thoughts about the death of Isabel Santos.

Claire drove through the town of Bernalillo. The cemetery wasn't where she thought it should have been—beside Our Lady of Sorrows Church. It was below the on-ramp to the Interstate. It didn't seem like a very desirable location, but the cemetery was established long before the Interstate. She had seen it many times but had never stopped. She turned off the side road from Route 44. Just past the cemetery a lot full of trailers advertised with a large sign that it was having a sale. The sign was tied to the fence and snapped in the breeze.

Claire parked and entered the cemetery surprised by the bright reds, pinks and yellows of the artificial flowers that covered the graves. She'd been expecting a duller, grayer place.

She liked to visit old graveyards; she saw them as an illustrated collection of poetry and short stories. Stories could be found in the names and dates of the departed: the men who had survived wars, the men who hadn't, the women who had died in childbirth, the children who had died young, the people who lived to a ripe old age even in the hardest of times. People didn't live any longer now than they ever had but a higher percentage of them lived to an advanced age. There was art in the symbols carved into the more elaborate tombstones—the birds, the crosses, the intertwined wedding rings—art in the ceramic figures left behind and in the weathered wood of the oldest markers. Poetry could be found in the epitaphs, many of which were in Spanish. Claire saw *juntos para siempre* (together forever), *descance en paz* (rest in peace), and one she especially liked, *si para el mundo eras uno, para nosotros eras el mundo* (for the world he was one, for us he was the world).

It was intriguing to think her ashes would eventually be scattered in the water or the wind, blending into the elements without a marker now that she no longer had a husband to lie beside in eternity. It would also be reassuring to be buried in a family plot beside her mother and father, her grandparents and the generations before them, people she never knew but would always be related to by the substance of her bones. Someday, if her children made no deeper connections in the course of their lives, they might lie next to her, too. This cemetery celebrated family and she envied the people here who would be *juntos para siempre*. But for her it was a dream. Her family had been in America almost as long as the

Santoses, but the Reyniers had never settled in one place long enough to have a family plot that went back several generations. Reyniers were scattered across the country from New York to Arizona. Unless Claire was willing to start her own dynasty, for her it would be the water or the wind.

But the Santoses were deeply rooted in New Mexico and Bernalillo, and Isabel would be buried near her ancestors. Claire went to her grave and found it marked with a brand new tombstone. Isabel Santos, it said, *descance en paz*. Hearts were carved into the stone, but Claire would have preferred the symbol of a butterfly. The artificial flowers on the grave were the right color—dark red, the color Isabel wore when she visited CSWR. A pebble sat on top of her tombstone. There were other people in the cemetery, but their attention was focused on the newly departed, not on Claire. She picked up the pebble and balanced it in her hand, thinking that holding it might tell her something, that being tactile would be better than being intellectual or emotional. It was hard not to get emotional at Isabel's grave, thinking she had already begun the process of turning to dust, hard not to feel that if she had only been in her office when Isabel called, if the document had been safely stored at the center, her death might have been prevented.

Claire took strength from the solidity of stone. Did people put pebbles on graves because stone endured? She knew people who collected stones because they liked the color or the markings or because a stone reminded them of a place they had been. The pebble in her hand was an ordinary gray stone crisscrossed by white lines, but if she stared at the lines hard enough and long enough, they took on the shape of mist and clouds. She replaced the pebble, trying to put it exactly where she had found it.

Her hand dropped to the top of the tombstone and she let it rest there, saying a final good-bye to Isabel Santos, whispering, "Rest in peace. *Descance en paz*. If there is anything I can do to make sense of your death, I will."

Other members of the Santos family were buried near Isabel. Most had tombstones with names, dates, a cross and *descance en paz* chiseled into them. The names Ester, Isabel, Manuel and Jesus occurred several times. Sometimes Claire came across families and couples buried together. Isabel's parents had died within two years of each other and their cross was marked with intertwined wedding rings and the epitaph *juntos para siempre*. Sometimes individuals were buried alone. There were other tombstones with pebbles on them. While she stared at the Santos tombstones she heard the trailer sign flap-flapping in the wind.

She moved away from this section and wandered into the far corners of Our Lady of Sorrows Cemetery where the markers were older and more primitive. Wooden crosses were attached to the fence or lay on the ground. If they had ever been inscribed, the inscriptions had weathered away. It made it difficult to tell how far back the cemetery went. The oldest dates Claire found were nuns who were buried here in the 1880's. It made her wonder where all the bodies from the 1600's and 1700's were.

A jackrabbit jumped out of the weeds and stared at her. In the very back corner Claire found the tombstone of Isabel Santos de Suazo, who also died young in 1890. Twenty years later her husband Moises Suazo was buried beside her. This was the oldest Santos tombstone in the cemetery. It had no cross. This tombstone was decorated with an open flower with six petals. There were lines in the middle of it that looked like musical notes arranged in the shape of a W. It was either a stamen or a symbol that Claire couldn't read. Scratched beneath the flower she saw the curved arms of a candlestick. This etching was rougher and lighter than the professionally carved flower and looked as if it had been added later by hand.

When she was back in her rental car Claire sketched the markings she had seen on a piece of paper. Then she drove to the police station to ask about her truck.

chapter twenty

Romero didn't have his own office. He shared a room with several other detectives. Phones were ringing, people were talking, but Claire felt he tuned it all out and focused on her. His eyes were warm and sympathetic.

"How is your arm?" he asked.

"Fine," she said.

"You'll get your truck back soon," he said. "The SUV must have tapped your truck's tail end as you went into the field. We found some paint marks that could help to identify it. We're checking Atencio's family and homeboys to see if any of them own a matching vehicle."

"Were the paint samples gray or black?"

"Black."

"Manuel Santos owns an SUV." Chuy had said that vehicle was gray, but Claire wasn't sure she believed him.

"How do you know that?" Romero asked.

"Chuy told me. I went by there this afternoon." Claire didn't consider it her civic duty to tell Romero that Tey Santos had been sipping marijuana stems she raised in her vegetable garden.

"I'll look into it," Romero said.

Although Claire hoped he would, she wasn't convinced; a wall seemed to go up whenever she mentioned the name of Manuel Santos, possibly because he was a local boy who had made good. "I asked Tey if someone had been in the house and covered the mirrors. She said she did."

"That the kind of thing *abuelas* do."

"Did you ask your grandmother about it?"

"Not yet."

"She told me she lit candles while she was in the house. She leaves the door unlocked; she says there is nothing left to steal. Tey thinks Tony Atencio is a very bad boy and that he killed Isabel." It seemed only fair to pass that on.

Romero made no comment.

"She said she would ask Manuel about comparing their DNA to the old bones, but I'm sure he'll say no."

"We can't make them unless we can establish that the old bones will help solve the current crime. Considering that the bodies are separated by four hundred years it's a very long shot."

"I know," Claire said. "After I left Tey's I went to the cemetery to see Isabel's grave. Someone had put a pebble on top of her tombstone. Is that one of the old ways, too?"

"I don't know." He shrugged. "Maybe in the old days when people were too poor to afford flowers they brought stones."

"Maybe," said Claire. "I came across the tombstone of another Isabel Santos who died in eighteen ninety. That one had flowers and a candlestick carved into the stone. Have you ever heard of her or the man she was married to, Moises Suazo?"

"No. How's the rental car working out?"

"All right."

"I'll give you a call when the truck is ready." He stood up signaling that the meeting was over.

"Thanks," Claire said.

She drove home through Sandia Pueblo where the road was lined with the faces of wildflowers. Recent rains had rejuvenated them, but even when it hadn't rained for months flowers bloomed in New Mexico. It could be a harsh place, but from May to November there were wildflowers beside the roads. Anyone who couldn't afford to buy artificial flowers could easily pick real flowers. But real flowers didn't last. Stones and artificial flowers did. Was that why people put them on graves?

She poured herself a glass of Chardonnay when she got home, took it into the living room, sat down on the sofa, and stared out the window at the Sandias where the piñon and juniper were sprouting shadows. She had a phone call to make and she wanted to have her thoughts in order before she did. It was early evening here, nighttime where she was calling. She didn't have the home phone number of the person she hoped to reach, but she got it from information. She hoped he would be home and wouldn't consider this an intrusion. She hoped she wouldn't wake him up.

"Hello," he answered in the grouchy tone of an animal disturbed in its lair.

"Harold. This is Claire Reynier."

"Oh," he replied. "And how are *you*?" The grouchiness disappeared from his voice. Harold Marcus seemed genuinely pleased to hear from her.

"I'm good. I hope I didn't wake you."

"No, it's only nine o'clock here and it's Saturday night. I can't go to bed at nine o'clock on Saturday even when I have nothing better to do. What's on your mind?"

"Have you learned any more about the skeleton?"

"Well, let's see, bone chemistry indicates he's a Caucasian. He died in the early seventeenth century when he was in his thirties, apparently of natural causes. I don't have the results back on the tooth enamel so I can't tell you where he grew up. The logical choices would be Spain or Mexico."

"I went to the Bernalillo cemetery today to visit Isabel Santos's grave. Someone had placed a pebble on top of her tombstone."

"That's interesting." Claire only had his voice to go on, but Harold seemed fully awake now. "It's an old Jewish custom to leave a stone at a grave."

"Why do they do that?"

"It's a sign that someone has been there."

"I found the grave of a woman named Isabel Santos who died in eighteen ninety and was married to a man named Moises Suazo."

"It's a Catholic cemetery, isn't it?"

"Yes."

"Catholics aren't likely to name their children Moses."

"The tombstone didn't have a cross but an etching of an open flower with a stamen in the middle that might be a symbol or a letter. I drew a picture."

"Can you fax me a copy?"

"Yes."

"How many petals did the flower have?"

"Six."

Claire heard the excitement of discovery in his voice. "I've seen similar flowers in other Sephardim cemeteries. It could be a representation of a six-pointed star. The Star of David appears on Jewish tombstones although in the past a six-pointed star wasn't exclusively a Jewish symbol."

"I also saw a candelabra carved on the tombstone, although it was lighter and rougher that the other carving. It may have been added later by hand."

"How many arms did the candelabra have?"

"Nine."

"That could make it a menorah. It would appear that Isabel the Saint married Moses the Jew. In the nineteenth century Ashkenazi Jewish merchants settled in New Mexico, but Suazo is a Spanish or Portuguese name, which would make Moises a Sephardic Jew. Nowadays when there are interfaith marriages, all too often the man forgets he's a Jew and takes the religion of his wife. That's one reason there are so few of us. But the tombstone would suggest that Isabel was the one who converted. Did they leave any heirs?"

"I didn't see any children buried nearby. Isabel Suazo died when she was only twenty-two. Chuy Santos sent me to his grandmother's house last night. Someone ran me off the ditch road into a tree in Isabel's yard."

"Were you hurt?"

Claire considered her bruised arm. "Not really, but my truck was damaged. I thought I saw a light in Isabel's house when I drove by. After the accident I went into the house with the police. Candles had been burning and the mirrors were covered in black. I went to the grandmother's today and she told me she had covered the mirrors and left candles burning in the house."

"Jews burn Shabbat candles on Friday nights to mark the beginning of the Sabbath. Covering the mirrors in black after a death is an old Jewish custom. Mourners are not supposed to be thinking about vanity. Mourning is only supposed to last for ten days, but people here may have lost sight of that. What is the grandmother's name?"

"Tey."

"That could be a diminutive of Ester, and Esther was the Hebrew Queen of Persia."

Claire liked to hear his excitement grow and know that someone else shared the joy of discovery.

"There were several Ester Santoses in the cemetery."

"Here's what I think," he continued. "I think Isabel Santos married into a Jewish family. Somehow the last words of Joaquín Rodriguez ended up in the hands of the Santos family, maybe through the Suazos. The Rodriguezes and the Suazoses could be related. Both names have a Portuguese connection and some of the Sephardim went to Portugal before emigrating to the New World."

"Have you learned any more about the cross?" Claire asked.

"It was made in Mexico in the late sixteenth century. It's from the same period as the bones, but so far that's the only way we can connect them. It's possible the bones belong to a Suazo and the Santos family moved into a Suazo house."

"There's another possibility." Claire's mind had leapt ahead of Harold Marcus's, but she'd had more time to think about what she'd learned in the cemetery. She was in New Mexico looking at the mountains that inspired big thoughts, whereas he was likely to be in a suburban house where the only view was of his backyard. She had learned when solving problems related to her work that sometimes it was best to return to the premises that had been taken for granted and reexamine them. "Suppose the first Manuel Santos to arrive in New Mexico was connected to Joaquín Rodriguez and brought the cross and the document with him. Maybe the Santoses were Jews before they came to New Mexico. Maybe the marriage between Isabel and Moises was an intrafaith marriage."

"Well, all the forensic techniques in the world won't tell me whether the skeleton belonged to a man who was circumcised. Strontium testing of tooth enamel could tell me if he spent time in Portugal as a boy. If he did, it would be an indication of Judaism, but it wouldn't be proof. And the question remains, how do you explain the family having the name of a saint and an Inquisitor?"

"I can't," Claire said. "But I'll keep trying."

"I'll do what I can to speed things along here. Do you think the Santos family has been telling you all they know?"

"Not entirely."

"Perhaps if you tell Tey what you've discovered, she'll tell you the whole truth."

"Perhaps," Claire said.

She said good-bye to Harold, hung up the phone and went to her window. The shadows on the mountain had begun to merge with the twilight. Soon the creatures of the night would be slipping out of their nests and their dens—the owls, the bats, the snakes and coyotes. In Harold's mind there was a line between truth and untruth and the methodological method could put the facts into one column or another. But that wasn't the way Tey Santos would look at things.

chapter twenty-one

Claire revisited Tey the following morning while the bells of Our Lady of Sorrows called the people of Bernalillo to church. She expected Manuel to be at the service but not Tey. She didn't know where Chuy would be, although the casino was always a possibility.

When she pulled into the yard, she was relieved not to see his truck. Tey was in the garden among corn stalks that were taller than she was. To be able to maintain a house and a garden at the age of ninety-two was a major accomplishment. Claire attributed Tey's long life to living in and caring for this fertile spot.

She stopped tending the corn and leaned on her cane when she saw Claire. "*Hola*," she called. "It's a beautiful morning." She didn't seem at all surprised that Claire had returned.

"*Hola*," said Claire. "Do you have any time to talk to me?"

"I have nothing left but time," Tey said. She maneuvered her way out of the corn stalks and headed for a bench parked under the willow tree. Claire followed and sat down beside her. The temperature was already in the nineties, but it was ten degrees cooler in the shade of the tree. Willows drew a lot of water and were rare in New Mexico. This one seemed to be converting ground water into a waterfall as the leaves cascaded around them creating a sheltered, private place, a good place to share a secret.

"You have a lot left," Claire said. "You have a house, a garden, a dog, a family."

"*Verdad*," Tey said. "And God gave me this nice tree to sit under."

"It's lovely here." Claire could have easily spent the morning exchanging pleasantries with Tey, but she was afraid Chuy would show up and there were things she preferred to say when he wasn't around.

"I went to the cemetery after I left here yesterday to pay my respects to Isabel," she began. "Someone had placed a pebble on top of her tombstone."

Tey's black eyes were alert, but she said nothing.

"I walked around the graveyard and came across graves for Isabel Santos de Suazo and Moises Suazo. They shared a tombstone and it had a six-pointed flower carved on it with a symbol inside. When I got home I called a friend who is Jewish." She had decided not to mention the Smithsonian at this point, thinking that the institutional connection might put Tey off. "He told me that he has seen similar flowers on Jewish tombstones, that it is an old Jewish custom to leave a stone at a grave."

"What else did he tell you?" Tey asked, clutching the top of her cane.

"It is also a Jewish custom to light candles on Friday nights to mark the Sabbath and to cover the mirrors when someone dies. That Tey is a nickname for the Hebrew name Esther."

Tey seemed to be stepping into the truth and blinking

her eyes at the light. She said without hesitation, "*Somos Judios.*" We are Jews. "I am named for Queen Esther. That name has been in my family forever."

It was where Claire's investigations had been leading, but she was so startled to hear Tey say so that she felt the bench was tipping and spilling her into deep water.

"Our ancestors were Jews," Tey said. "Sometimes we named a son Jesus so no one would know. For years we always married Jews, but now there are hardly any left. The make-believe Catholics became real Catholics. If those bones under the house belong to our ancestor, they are the bones of a Jew. But that's all I know. I don't know anything about Manuel Santos before he came here. I don't know why he had the name of a saint and an Inquisitor. I never heard of Joaquín Rodriguez until Isabel told you about that piece of paper."

"Did Isabel know you are Jewish?"

"No. I am the only one who knows that now. When I die the secrets go with me. The women pass on the religion and the tradition of the Jews. When they are old enough, we tell the young women, but Isabel died before I could tell her. Now there is nobody left to tell."

"Chuy and Manuel don't know?"

"No. They may think they know a little, but they don't know everything."

"Would Manuel be upset to find out? He's a devout Catholic, isn't he? Wouldn't it be hard now to think of himself as a Jew?"

"It would be hard," Tey agreed. "Because his wife is very Catholic. At first the Jews had to pretend to be Catholic. We could lose our land or our life if anyone found out. But as time went by some people became real Catholics and forgot where they came from. Some families gave a son to the church so

162

the church wouldn't know they were Jews. If you could read, they thought you were a Jew. We were called the people of the book. If a son became a priest he could read the Old Testament and bring it home. In the old days when they were both in hiding from the friars, the Penitentes let the Jews practice in their moradas. They chanted in the old language."

"Do you ever want to go to a synagogue and connect with the Ashkenazi Jews?"

"No," Tey said. "It's not the same. They are white people who drive big cars. We have been hiding from the church, lighting candles, speaking the old language, never eating pork, sweeping to the middle of the room, practicing the old ways, doing things in secret for four hundred years. We are not like the other Jews. It hurts me when I hear other Jews are hurt and killed. *Adonay es mi dio*. His words are in my heart. I am part of them, but I am different. It's too late to change that."

"I could put you in touch with my Jewish friend Harold Marcus at the Smithsonian. I know he would love to talk to you."

"I don't want to talk to him. I don't want to talk to anybody. I am only telling you this because you are a woman I can pass my story on to and you knew my Isabelita. There is a mezuzah in her house, very old. Would you like to see it?"

Claire supposed mezuzah was a Hebrew word, but she didn't know what it meant. "What is it?" she asked.

"It's a little box with a prayer inside." Tey gripped the top of her cane and prepared to push herself off from the bench. "Let's walk. It's a nice day."

"Are you sure?" Claire asked. "I'll be happy to drive."

"No. It's good to walk. I say His words sometimes when I walk along the road."

Tey stood up and led the way, refusing any help as she climbed the ditch bank. Her pace was steady as a tortoise but much slower than the pace Claire kept when she walked. She checked her impatience by cranking up her powers of observation. The ditch road was shaded by the branches of cottonwoods. The sun broke through the leaves and dappled the path, giving it the shifting reality of a pointillist painting. The weeds were high beside the ditch. The sun hadn't touched the wild pink morning glories yet and they were still in bloom. A duck flapped its wings and lifted out of the ditch, which was brown and muddy from the recent rains. Claire could see the water ripple and hear it lap against the banks. They came to the carcass of a dead bird in the road. Tey stopped and poked it with her walking stick.

"A coyote did that," she said. "They come here at night. When my dog hears them he cries and asks to come inside."

The ditch was a watering hole, where animals came to drink, to eat and get eaten. During the night it was wild and dangerous, a place where Claire herself had felt hunted. But in the morning it was green, fertile and peaceful, far removed from the noise and danger of the street. Along here nothing appeared to have changed for centuries. Claire was glad they had taken this walk so she could remember the ditch as it appeared now and not as a place where an SUV had pursued her in the rain.

After her comment about the coyotes, Tey kept silent and focused on picking her way down the dusty road. As they approached the old house Claire offered her arm and helped her down the path that led to the embankment. The rain had washed away any tracks. As soon as she was on level ground again Tey let go of Claire's arm. They walked to the door. Tey took keys from her pocket and unlocked it.

"Chuy locked the house yesterday," she said. "We can't leave it open any more with all those bad boys around."

The light was dim inside the house, but Claire could see that the mirrors were still covered.

"The closet door is open," Tey said. "Was it open when you were here?"

"Yes."

"It was closed when I left. I always keep it closed." She went to the closet, reached around the door and slid her right hand along the inside of the doorjamb. "The prayer is supposed to be on the door post of the house, but my grandmother hid it here. It's gone," she cried. "Our little mezuzah is gone. Look."

She placed Claire's hand against the doorjamb, and she felt a hollow section a few inches long carved out of the wood.

"The mezuzah had a prayer inside that kept this house safe. And now my Isabelita is dead and the mezuzah is gone. This is not a place for people to live anymore."

"Was it still here after Isabel died?"

"Yes. I felt it Friday when I lit the candles."

"Did Chuy or Manuel know about it?"

"No. It's hidden here. You can't find it unless you know where to look." Tey made her way to the sofa and sank into the cushions. Claire felt that the spirit that had kept her so fierce and strong was escaping along with the dust from the cushions.

"Help me find out who took it," Claire said. "It could be the person who ran me off the road. It could be Isabel's killer."

"You think we are related to this Joaquín?" Tey asked.

"I don't know if you are related, but I think you are connected in some way. You used the same phrase Joaquín used: *'Adonay es mi dio'*."

"It's what my mother said, *descance en paz.* Why didn't my Isabelita show me what she found? Why did she tell you and that May Brennan?"

"Maybe she didn't have time to show it to you." It was a lame explanation, but the only one Claire could offer at the moment.

Tey's tired shrug implied she didn't believe it either. "That May came to see me once to ask me about the grave of Isabel Suazo, but I wouldn't tell her anything. It was none of her business. You think those bones that were under the floor will tell us something?" she asked.

"They might."

"Okay. Go ahead. Take my blood, do your tests. Find out what you need to know." She pulled up her sleeve and offered a scrawny bare arm to Claire.

"Someone else will have to do the tests," Claire said.

"I will tell Chuy and Manuel the family story. They're big boys; it's time they knew. No one is going to take our land now. You find out what happened to my Isabelita. You think she was killed for being a Jew? They stopped killing us for that long ago."

"I don't think she was killed for that. I think she was killed because someone wanted the document she found, but the police want to believe it was Tony Atencio. You need to go to them. Tell them everything. Tell them about the mezuzah. Detective Romero is a local boy. He knows something about the old ways."

"What is his first name?"

"Jimmy."

"I think I know Adela, his grandmother. Okay, I will call him."

"Let me get my car and drive you back to the house."

166

"Okay," Tey said.

"Will you be all right here? Do you want me lock the door?"

"I'll be all right. What can anybody do to me now? I heard about an old woman in Chama. A bear came into her house looking for food and killed her. To be killed by a bear or a robber—what's the difference? When you're old, dying in your own house is not a bad way to go." She thumped her cane against the floor. "If that robber comes back, I'll make him sorry he killed my Isabelita."

"I'll be back soon," Claire said.

She hurried along the ditch, too busy thinking about Tey to notice much except that the sun had landed on the wild morning glories and the blossoms had shriveled.

Tey had moved outside and was sitting under the portal when Claire returned. She seemed to have regained some of her spirit. "Not my day to be killed by a bear or a robber," she said.

When Claire dropped her off at the other house she said, "You find that killer for me."

"I'll do my best," Claire said, "but you need to call the police."

"Okay," said Tey.

As she drove home through the Sandia Pueblo Claire thought how often one generation forgets the past leaving the next to search and reinvent. If knowledge was passed down from one generation to the next, she would know all about her own ancestors. As it was, she knew next to nothing. She liked the phrase "people of the book" and identified with it. Not because she had a Jewish connection. When the Reyniers fled Europe they were persecuted for being Protestants and by now they were very lapsed Protestants. But Claire was a book person who turned to the written word for solace and for answers. The question she needed to answer was whether Isabel had been killed because the Santoses were people of the book. The long arm of the Inquisition could not have reached out of the past to punish Isabel in the twenty-first century, but there might have been some other connection. Had Isabel learned the Santoses were descended from Jews, and was that what she called to tell Claire? Was she intending to bring the cross and the document to the center? Could someone else have learned of the connection like May Brennan, Peter Beck, Warren Isles, or her own brothers? Could Joaquín Rodriguez's last words have remained somewhere in Isabel's house? Had someone gone back to the house for the document or the mezuzah, been surprised by Claire, and run her off the road? Did that someone know she was coming?

It might hurt Manuel's standing with the Church and his career to have his Jewish background come out, but would he kill his own sister to suppress that information? Maybe he had meant to warn and not to kill. Maybe Isabel had fallen and hit her neck during a struggle over the document. Claire hadn't had any physical altercations with her own brother as an adult, but they'd had plenty when they were growing up.

She visualized the same scenario with Isabel's other brother. Suppose Chuy found out about the document, learned it was valuable and needed money to pay off his gambling debts? Isabel refused to give it to him and they struggled. If the document had been sold, it might be hidden but at least it would be preserved.

Claire wondered how the police would react to learning that the Santoses had a hidden Jewish connection. Romero was more likely to find it relevant than his boss. Claire had to consider whether she had any business pursuing a line of investigation if the Sandoval County Sheriff's Department rejected it. Was it egotism on her part to think her experience and knowledge could ask and answer questions they could not?

CHAPTER twenty-two

When she got home, she turned on the cooler, let the cat out, took the documents August had given her to her courtyard and set them on the banco. Before she began to read she picked the dead flowers from her datura, which grew faster with less encouragement than any plant she had ever seen. A few summer showers and it covered the floor of her courtyard and climbed the wall. On the night of the full moon she had as many as fifty flowers. As the tendrils approached her front door, she had the sensation that one night they would turn the knob, slither into the house and down the hallway, enter her bedroom and wrap themselves around her neck in the same way the Inquisition had reached out of the past.

It was one hundred degrees or more in the courtyard. The sun had been beating on the adobe walls all morning. The bricks soaked up the heat and reflected it back at Claire. She went into the kitchen and poured herself a lemonade with ice. She took the drink outside and sat down in a sliver of shade in the corner where the banco met the house.

Last night's white satin datura flowers turned brown and

shriveled in the heat and the light of the sun, yet the plant had to absorb the sun's energy in the daytime to blossom at night. Mystics of many religions had gone into the desert to find their visions in the dryness and the heat. But the temperature in the desert dropped thirty degrees once the sun went down. What happened to a mystic's vision in the darkness? Did it blossom into something pure and white or did it develop long tendrils that reached out to garrote the nonbeliever?

What Claire disliked about religion was that the burning heat of vision too often turned into a heated passion for destruction. She thought about all the slaughter that had been carried out in the name of the God she knew, the Christian God: the Jews and Muslims garroted and burned at the stake, the millions of Indians killed during the Conquest. It had happened elsewhere in the names of other gods, but she knew more about this part of the world. She knew all the ways in which the Conquest had been despicable. What kind of a God would allow millions of people to be slaughtered in his name? It was not a God she could connect with.

She sipped her lemonade, sank deeper into the shadow and read through the documents, fascinated once again by the relationship language had to events. In this case elegant language described horrific events. She read that Joaquín Rodriguez was "relaxed to the secular arm" and led through the streets on a "saddled horse". Someone stepped out of the crowd and Joaquín spoke words interpreted as repentance and conversion. He was garroted until he appeared dead then burned to a cinder. The events were witnessed by Manuel Santos, among others. Claire wondered about the sincerity of the conversion that allowed the Church to strangle Joaquín before they burned him. Was it a true conversion or a convenience that allowed the church to save face? She wondered about the relationship between Manuel Santos, the Inquisitor, and Manuel Santos, the settler. Manuel Santos the Inquisitor, had to be a Catholic in good standing. Manuel Santos the settler, had been a pretend Catholic. What was the connection between the Santos men and Joaquín Rodriguez? Why had Joaquín's last words turned up hidden inside a cross under a house owned by the Santos family? The Spanish kept detailed records of everything they did, but to find a particular record could take months of searching through archives written by hand in a language in which Claire was not fluent. She looked through the other papers August had given her. Raquel had gone to her death at the stake screaming at the Inquisitors. Daniel was never tried; too young perhaps, to be judged by the Inquisition.

Another place to turn was the scholar Peter Beck's exhaustive, pedantic, duller-than-dust study, which should be on the shelves at Zimmerman. She put that off till the next day, went inside and called Harold Marcus.

"Hello," he said. "What's it like out there?"

"Hot."

"Ah, for the dry heat. It's so humid here I feel like I'm swimming. If only I had gills. Did you talk to Tey Santos?"

"Yes."

"And?"

"You were right. Tey is a diminutive for Ester. She lit the candles, covered the mirror and put the pebble on the tombstone. A mezuzah hidden in a closet in Isabel's house disappeared, and she showed me the hollow in the doorjamb where it had been. She admitted that the Santoses are Jews."

The line crackled as if an electrical storm danced somewhere between NM and DC. "I knew it. The symbol you saw in the flower on Isabel Suazo's grave could be a shin."

"What's that?"

"It's the twenty-second letter of the Hebrew alphabet and first letter of shema, the prayer Jews say. It means 'Hear O Israel, the Lord is our God, the Lord is One.' Tey Santos is living history. I want to meet her, bring along a tape recorder, record her experiences while she is still alive. Can you arrange it?"

The scientist in Harold had surfaced, eager to put Tey under a microscope. "It's a very personal, private matter," Claire said. "Tey's family has been practicing their religion in secret for hundreds of years. It's not something that's easy for her to talk about. She doesn't see much relationship between her religion and modern-day Judaism although she does feel a connection to the Jewish people."

"She's an incredible resource. We can't let her go to waste."

Actually she's a person, not a resource, thought Claire, not someone you want to subject to the methodological method. "She won't agree to talk to you." Her voice assumed the deep freeze tone WASPs used to put people in their place. "The religion is passed down from woman to woman in the Santos family. One reason Tey talked to me is that I am a woman. She wasn't able to tell the story to Isabel before she died, so she told it to me. I'd be violating a confidence if I sent you to talk to her. She used the same phrase Joaquín Rodriguez did, by the way— *Adonay es mi dio.*"

"God in the Spanish singular. The Sephardic Jews were willing to speak the name of God out loud."

"She said sometimes they named a son Jesus as protective cover. Her grandson is named Jesus."

"They named boys Adonay, too. You don't see people naming their son God in English."

"She told me the Jews were known as the people of the book."

"We followed the Old Testament. There was a time when it was considered a sign of Judaism to be able to read," Harold said.

"You'll be happy to know that she agreed to a DNA test."

"That's good. We'll know then whether she's related to the old bones. I'll set it up with the OMI. We still won't know for sure whether the skeleton is Manuel Santos, but it would be a reasonable assumption given the date of the bones."

Reasonable assumption wasn't enough for Claire. "I want to know for sure. I want to know how Joaquín Rodriguez's last words ended up under the floor of Isabel Santos's house. I want to know if there's a connection between the two Manuel Santoses. Is there anyone there who could help?" The Smithsonian was the place people turned to for American history, but she didn't know what information they'd be able to provide about the Mexican Inquisition.

"I'll ask around and see what I can find out," Harold Marcus said.

"Thanks," Claire replied.

She hung up the phone and stared out her window at the piñon-studded mountains wanting to share her discovery with someone who would understand how much it meant to her. She had visited Barcelona with Pietro, sighed with him under the Bridge of Sighs, walked along Las Ramblas and down a narrow *calle* lined with the fluid shapes of an Antoni Gaudi building, gone to the house of the alchemist, explored the old Jewish quarter without finding any trace of

Sephardim. Barcelona was a city that kept its secrets, which was one of the things she liked about it.

She went to her computer, opened a file and composed an E-mail. "Pietro," it began.

"I've discovered that the Santos family is descended from conversos. Their ancestry must go back to Medieval Spain. They have been living in New Mexico and practicing Judaism in secret for four hundred years. It has been a wonderful discovery for me."

Her eyes returned to the window. What to say next?

"Do you remember the time we spent in Barcelona searching for the Jewish quarter. Kissing under the Bridge of Sighs, going to the harbor to see the statue of Columbus and imagining his voyage to the end of the world? Do you ever wish we could go back there again?"

It wasn't the appropriate communication to send to a man with a sick wife. And if someday his wife were to die was not a thought she should allow to enter her mind. There were times when being a WASP woman felt like being shipwrecked on a remote and vacant island. She couldn't imagine Pietro's life in Italy would ever be a vacant island. Full of family and chaos, maybe, but never empty.

As E-mail was not an exact science and anything written had the possibility of being inadvertently sent, Claire deleted her message, and turned toward the window. The sky remained an unfettered blue. If it was going to rain the thunderheads would be building by now. She picked up the phone to call John Harlan, who knew something about remote islands of the heart, but she changed her mind, put the phone down, went outside and followed a path that led through the foothills into the mountains. Eventually it reached the top of the peaks, but she only went to the elevation where high desert cactus segued into piñon/juniper forest. She sat down on a favorite rock and stared at the line where piñon and juniper turned to stone at a higher elevation. Her eyes focused on that spot while her mind focused on the empty place where people turned to God.

chapter twenty-three

When she got to work in the morning she looked up *The Inquisition in Mexico* by Peter Beck on the computer. There were numerous books on the Inquisition in general but few on the Mexican Inquisition. She wrote down the call number for Peter's book. That afternoon she walked through the stacks following the numbers until she came to the B's and Peter Beck. His book turned up exactly where it was supposed to. It was a massive volume, heavy enough to serve as a weapon.

After dinner that evening she down on her sofa and opened Peter Beck's exhaustive and exhausting opus. She went first to the copyright page and learned that this was a first edition published ten years ago. It had remained the definitive study, still in use as a textbook, still earning a royalty for Peter Beck. She turned next to the last page to see how long it was—1235 pages. Each one of these pages was packed with the small, dense print of a university press book. No space breaks, no dialogue, no white space on the page. The length was formidable, the subject depressing, the style stultifyingly dull. There were many things she would rather be doing than reading Peter Beck's plodding prose—washing the dishes, watching the news, vacuuming the carpet, polishing her silver, talking to her cat.

An index made the job easier. There was an extensive bibliography listing sources in Hebrew, Spanish, Portuguese, Latin, French, German and English establishing that Peter Beck's knowledge was encyclopedic and his scholarship impeccable. Claire skimmed through the bibliography encountering one of her all-time favorite books—*History of the Conquest of Mexico and History of the Conquest of Peru* by the nearly blind scholar William Prescott. He had marvelous material to work with—criminals and kings, Cortes and Montezuma, Pizarro and Atahuallpa, rooms full of beaten gold ornaments, captives with their still warm hearts ripped from their chests. Prescott's imaginative and evocative style did it justice.

Peter Beck's material wasn't quite as marvelous and it demonstrated the cruelest, most self-righteous and inhumane side of human behavior. His material had the potential to be revealing and interesting, but his style got in the way. Claire consulted the index and turned to the first entry of the name Rodriguez on page 562. It was at this point that Joaquín's uncle Tomás arrived in the New World and quickly established himself as a trader. He petitioned the court to bring in family members from Portugal and Spain to expand his trading network. The request was granted even though the Rodriguezes were a known converso family. The crown was willing to overlook their ancestry as long as Tomás remained useful to them. The family members he brought to Mexico included Ester, Raquel, Joaquín and Daniel, the wife and children of Tomás's deceased brother David who had lived in Portugal. Unfortunately for the family, Tomás became too successful.

Fearing his power and coveting his wealth, the Inquisition arrested him in 1594, confiscating his property and letting him languish in jail until he died of natural causes.

Joaquín Rodriguez came under suspicion as soon as Tomás was arrested. He was questioned then released. A year later he was arrested again when a neighbor accused him of being a fervent Judaizer. Joaquín learned at age fifteen that his ancestry was Jewish and he became passionate enough about it to circumcise himself in the Rio de los Remedios. He was tried for the crimes of heresy and apostasy at age twenty-five in 1595. He refused to repent, but eventually, under repeated torture on the rack, he gave up the names of his mother, Ester, his sister, Raquel, and his brother, Daniel. Raquel was twenty-two at the time and Daniel was sixteen. Raquel was burned at the stake in 1596. Joaquín and his mother were garroted. Daniel was considered too young to be tried for the crime of heresy and was assigned to the care of a Catholic family after his own family was incarcerated. That was the last entry Claire found for Daniel Rodriguez. She wondered whether his new family succeeded in turning him into a good Catholic. She wondered what effect seeing his family executed had on a sixteen-year-old boy.

It was the material of a soaring and epic novel but Peter's prose kept it grounded. Claire longed for the graceful similes and metaphors of Prescott or some of the flowery, elegant prose of the "Inquisition Case of Joaquín Rodriguez". She had read that document several times by now and she was sure that Peter had read it many more times. The only difference she found in his book was based on an eyewitness account that Claire hadn't seen. In this version Joaquín rode to his death on a saddled horse with a green cross tied between his hands. A young man stepped out of the crowd also holding a cross and embraced Joaquín. The two men spoke to each other in soft voices. As Joaquín was led to the burning ground, the young man confronted the witness Manuel Santos to tell him that Joaquín had repented and converted, which was enough to save him from being burned alive. The young man may have been known to Joaquín but his identity was never established. Between the lines Claire saw that the inability to identify him galled Peter Beck.

The Rodriguez martyrs—Joaquín, Ester and Raquel—were given a single chapter in a long and brutal history. The Inquisition continued with varying degrees of severity until the Mexican Revolution. There were long periods when crypto Jews were more or less ignored interspersed by times when they were actively persecuted. After this chapter the Rodriguez name did not appear again. No mention was made of Joaquín's last words, although Peter quoted liberally from his journals. The only Santos Claire found in the index was Manuel, the witness who became corregidor. His name reappeared from time to time until he participated in his last Inquisition in 1614, proving that he was not the same Manuel Santos who came north with Oñate's expedition.

Claire put down the book and checked her watch surprised to learn that it wasn't bedtime yet. She had expected to be kept awake well into the night, but the index made her job easier. Peter Beck had spent years on the Mexican Inquisition and had researched and written the definitive book. Still, it was impossible to answer every question relating to an *auto-de-fe* that went on for hundreds of years. She wondered if he had moved on to another project when he finished *The Inquisition in Mexico* or if he continued searching for previously undiscovered material, assuming he was willing to concede that there was any undiscovered material.

Even if he wasn't, people might have come to him with new information once the book was published.

As she still had an hour left before bedtime she decided to search the Internet to see if Peter or anyone else had come up with new material relating to Joaquín Rodriguez. She went to the Google search engine, typed in the name Joaquín Rodriguez and got 23,322 replies. The o's in Google stretched across her screen, each one representing a page of entries. Her allotted hour could extend to a week or a month if she let it. Scrolling through the list she discovered that many of the entries were in Spanish, some were in Portuguese, others were in French. Since Google offered instant translation Claire tried it out on a Portuguese entry; she found that language more difficult to read than either French or Spanish. Instant translator got the literal essence of the words but missed all subtleties of rhythm and meaning. Some of the mistakes were amusing. The overall clunkiness of the prose reminded Claire of Peter Beck's style. She visualized his brain as a computer program trying without success to imitate the subtlety of a human mind as it organized his voluminous research. A thought like this convinced her it was time to go to bed.

Nevertheless she continued scrolling through the list without opening any more websites. The beginning sentences told her if they were about Joaquín Rodriguez, the Jewish mystic who was killed by the Inquisition in 1596. She skipped ahead to page 20, then 30, then 40. The deeper she delved into the entries, the further removed the Joaquín Rodriguezes became from the Inquisition. She found doctors named Joaquín Rodriguez, students, writers, and on page 50 she found one who was a Colombian drug lord. It was sad to see the name of the poet and the mystic affixed to a drug dealer and to think the men might be distantly related. She moved on the very last o in "Google" and found a Joaquín Rodriguez who was a scientist in Sao Paulo, Brazil. Even on this page, however, she found listings for her Joaquín. In fact she had found him on every page she searched. To eliminate all entries she would have to search every page and look at all 23,322 of them. That was impossible, but she wasn't ready to stop either. She had the hunter's heightened awareness of being on the scent. The clock in the lower right hand corner of her computer screen was marking time but she avoided looking at it.

To narrow her search she added the name Manuel Santos to Joaquín Rodriguez. This time she only got a thousand hits and a number of them were references to articles Peter Beck had written. Some were entries on syllabi for courses he and others had taught. There were numerous websites, but she only found five articles. She opened them, read them, found nothing new.

Nemesis came into the room, meowed and rubbed against her leg saying it was past bedtime. She stopped for a minute and looked at the window. Had she gone outside she would have seen the distant warmth of the stars, but her window had the impermeable blackness of her computer screen after it was turned off. Except for the yellow light of her desk lamp, her room was dark, her house was dark. She was sure her neighbors' houses were also dark. Her office was a boat adrift on a sea of dark. She stretched, shook the sleep from her brain, said "in a minute" to Nemesis and started another search.

This time she entered the name of Daniel Rodriguez ending up with 20,200 entries, most of which belonged to a baseball player. Some were the same articles she had found in her previous search. It was getting later. She needed to narrow her search even further.

Giving it one last go-for-broke search before turning off the computer she combined the names Daniel Rodriguez, Joaquín Rodriguez, Manuel Santos and Peter Beck, which should have been complicated enough to eliminate all the o's from Google. To Claire's surprise she got a response, the URL for the syllabus of a course in Mexican history taught by a professor named Richard Joslin at Berkeley. On his supplemental reading list was an article titled "The Identity of the Man in the Crowd at the Inquisition of Joaquín Rodriguez" written by Peter Beck and published in the *Historical Journal of the Americas*, which Claire knew had lost its funding several years ago and was no longer being published. Professor Joslin had made a notation below the title saying "Daniel Rodriguez, Joaquín Rodriguez, Manuel Santos. An interesting theory, but the facts didn't support it." That remark struck Claire as the kind of not so subtle putdown at which academics excelled, although they were more likely to say it in class than put it in writing on the Internet. She knew Peter Beck would love to read that an article he published was not supported by fact. If it had been in his power he was likely to have deleted the notation and closed the website. She printed the page so she would have the information at hand in the morning. While she waited for it to print out she wondered about the upstart professor who would dare criticize Peter Beck on a syllabus, searched some more, and found he was no upstart but a man who'd had a long and distinguished career as a history professor before retiring from Berkeley.

She did another search using the title of the article but nothing else came up. She searched for the *Historical Journal of the Americas* but found no website. Apparently the journal had gone out of business before the Internet boom compelled scholars to put everything they had ever read or written on the web. She felt she had come to a wall as impermeable as the darkness of her window, and allowed herself to look down at her computer clock. Three thirty a.m., even later than she had expected. She was still burning with the fire of her computer chase, but she had to go to work tomorrow. She shut off the computer and went to bed wondering what Peter had discovered that earned him a put-down from a respected scholar.

chapter twenty-four

She spent the rest of the night chasing those thoughts around the bed, finally falling into a deep sleep a half hour before the alarm went off to jangle her awake. She climbed out of bed knowing she would face the day through the dull haze of exhaustion and her nerves would have a ragged edge. Lights would be too bright, noises too loud. People would violate the perimeter of her private space which extended a couple of feet beyond normal. She had to go to work. Staying up most of the night searching for a document was no excuse to take the day off. The best way to get through days like this was to keep the blinds drawn, the door shut, and do routine work on the computer. She had an extra cup of coffee before she left the house and another when she got to the center.

She was sitting at her desk staring at a blank computer screen trying to lasso a thought that remained out of reach when someone knocked at her door. She was tempted to ignore it and pretend she wasn't in, but the visitor knocked again.

"You in there?" Celia asked.

The one person Claire didn't mind seeing today was Celia. "I'm here," she said. "Come on in."

Celia swirled in wearing a black dress accented by a liquid silver necklace and a slew of silver bracelets. "What's up? You look like you were awake all night."

"Most of it," Claire replied.

"Doing what? Dancing? Snuggling?"

"I wish," said Claire. "It was a computer search." "You can do that all day. Nights are for snuggling and dancing." Celia made a cuddling motion and her arms rattled, making Claire wish she weren't wearing so many bracelets.

She had a husband to snuggle with. Claire did not. Even when Claire had a husband, he wasn't a snuggler. "I was hot on the trail of a document," she said.

"Did you find it?"

"Not exactly. Tey Santos told me on Sunday that her family is descended from crypto Jews. Her given name is Ester."

"That's an amazing discovery."

"I meant to tell you yesterday, but you were out. She still practices some of the old ways like lighting candles on Friday night and covering the mirrors when someone dies. She used the same phrase Joaquín Rodriguez did—*Adonay es mi dio*. Isabel died before Tey could pass the knowledge on to her. She took me back to Isabel's house to show me a mezuzah, but it had been stolen."

"That kind of information usually isn't shared with outsiders," Celia said. "Tey must have found you *simpatica*."

"It could be because I'm a woman and after Isabel died she didn't have anyone else to tell it to."

"You're a good listener. A rare skill these days."

"Am I?" Claire asked. In her tired state listening seemed like a skill that was beyond reach.

"Of course." Celia picked a paperweight from Claire's desk and balanced it in her hands. "What document were you looking for?"

"I read Peter Beck's book last night, the part about the Rodriguez family and the Inquisitor, Manuel Santos."

"*That* kept you up all night?"

"No, I was done by nine, but I came across something I hadn't known before. A cross was tied to Joaquín's hands as he was led through the crowd on the way to the *quemadero*. A young man holding another cross exchanged words with him and then he spoke to Manuel Santos. That event was interpreted as the conversion that saved Joaquín from being burned alive at the stake."

"The church would have interpreted a sneeze as a conversion at that point if it would save face."

"Maybe I was reading between the lines but it seemed to annoy Peter Beck that he wasn't able to identify the young man. I did a search and found an article he wrote titled *The Identity of the Man in the Crowd at the Inquisition of Joaquín Rodriguez* published in the *Historical Journal of the Americas*."

"That publication is history now. That's an article that would have been read by six people even when the journal was still being published."

"It makes it difficult to find. Here's the reference I found for it on the syllabus of a course taught at Berkeley." She handed the printout to Celia whose bracelets clinked as she reached across the desk to take it. "Don't you think it's unusual for a professor to criticize an article he recommends even if it is only on his supplemental reading list? He might be willing to say that in class but to put it in print?"

Celia read the syllabus. "It would be unusual for this professor. Richard Joslin was a wonderful man with a generous spirit, highly respected, but then he developed Alzheimer's and had to retire. It was a great loss to the department."

"Where is he now?"

"In a home somewhere, I'd say. Some kind of Alzheimer's theme park if he's lucky. Alzheimer's patients are happier if they live in an environment that reminds them of their past, someplace where they can eat comfort foods, wear bell bottoms or Bermuda shorts, and listen to the old songs."

"Maybe my own mind was gone in the middle of the night, but when I read in Peter's book that the young man embraced Joaquín, I had the thought that they exchanged crosses and the young man ended up with Joaquín's cross with his last written words stating that he would not convert to Catholicism." In the fuzzy haze of exhaustion the conclusion to that thought seemed to have lost the definition it had last night.

But Celia, wide awake and full of energy, reached the same conclusion. "And someone brought that cross to New Mexico and it ended up under Isabel Santos's floor?"

"Yes."

"Then who was the young man?"

"I wish I knew. Tey Santos agreed to DNA testing so eventually we will know if she is descended from the skeleton found under the floor. It's possible that person brought the cross to New Mexico, but how would you prove it? You can't get fingerprints from a skeleton. It will also be hard to determine whether that skeleton is Manuel Santos the settler or not, but if he turns out to be Tey's ancestor he's a crypto Jew. The question is how could there be a crypto Jew named Manuel Santos and an Inquisitor named Manuel Santos living in the same time and place? Even now it's not that common a name."

"Sometimes crypto Jews took the names of prominent citizens as protective cover."

"But the name of an Inquisitor?"

"Why don't you just call Peter Beck and ask him what he said in his article?"

"I don't trust him. I don't like him. He'll accuse me of inserting myself into his field. If he intended to tell me about the article, he had plenty of opportunity to do so the day I met him."

"He may have been embarrassed that his scholarship was challenged by Richard Joslin."

Claire wondered if Peter Beck was capable of embarrassment. "Maybe," she said. "There are other ways of finding the article."

"I'll see what I can do."

"Thanks."

Celia pushed her bracelets aside to consult her watch. "I have to go to a meeting. Talk to you later."

"Okay."

She left the office, shutting the door gently behind her, leaving Claire with the rest of the day to fill. Although she wanted to spend it entering boring data on the computer, she needed to track down Peter Beck's article. She thought about her datura plant putting out runners and creeping along the ground, opening its satiny blossoms to let bees, moths, hummingbirds, whatever happened to be flying through the night settle in. She needed to send out feelers herself.

First she put out a interlibrary loan request. Then she called Harold Marcus and told him her theory about the crosses. "Interesting," he said. "I'll see if anyone here can track down the article."

Then she called August Stevenson and asked him to keep an eye out for it. "Delighted to help," he said.

She wanted to talk to John Harlan, too, but decided to visit the store after work. The other people she needed to call—May Brennan and Detective Romero—were more problematic. She didn't know whether Tey had kept her promise and talked to Romero. Then there was the issue of why May hadn't told her she'd spoken to Tey about the grave of Isabel Suazo.

She dialed May's number at the Bernalillo Historical Society.

"Oh, Claire," May replied in a weary, put-upon voice. "How are you?"

"Fine," Claire replied, thinking her own voice was a blanket thrown over a teddy bear cholla.

"That's nice."

"I was with Tey Santos over the weekend and she told me you asked about Isabel Suazo's grave."

"It was a couple of years ago. She told me she was a good Catholic. I wasn't going to argue with her."

"Did you have any reason to argue with her?"

"Not really. I was just gathering information, that's all. People are always asking me for information about the crypto Jews. Isabel Santos married a Jew. I thought there might be some connection. Look, Claire, it's busy here. Can I call you back?"

"Please."

After that unproductive conversation, Claire called Detective Romero on his cell phone to ask if he had spoken to Tey Santos. "I got a message from her yesterday," he said. "But I haven't had a chance to go over there. I'll get back to you once I talk to her."

"Thanks."

That left Claire with nothing better to do than enter data onto the computer. She kept her door closed and her blinds drawn and at noon she put her head down on the desk and went to sleep. She woke up feeling her head had been screwed sideways. She stretched to get out the kinks, then she had lunch—another cup of coffee, an apple and a granola bar— and went back to entering data on the computer. At three she received a call saying there was someone at the information desk to see her. She walked out and found Detective Romero in his brown uniform.

"I happened to be in town," he said. "I hope you don't mind my stopping by."

"Of course not," said Claire. "Come into my office."

She led him down the hall and shut the door behind them, thinking this happened to be a good time to talk to Detective Romero. Her door and blinds had been closed all day. Whatever attention that would attract had already been attracted. She had inadvertently created an intimate atmosphere. As he sat down she remembered how relaxed Jimmy Romero looked in jeans and a T-shirt the night he drove her home. It was a thought she should have checked at the door.

"I called the mechanic before I left Bernalillo. Your truck will be ready in a day or two."

"Yay," Claire said.

"Getting tired of the rental car?" He smiled.

"Very."

"I went to see Tey Santos and she told me they are Marranos, which was why she lit the candles and covered the mirrors. She said her old ways are Marrano ways."

Claire tensed when she heard the word Marrano. Literally, it meant swine. Sometimes people used it in an ironic way to refer to themselves, but it was as derogatory as "nigger" or "wetback" or "beaner" or all the other insulting names people called each other. "She told me that, too. I thought you should know."

"When I talked to her before she was convinced that Tony Atencio had killed Isabel, but now she doesn't think so. What changed her mind?" He leaned back in his chair and his eyes lit on Claire.

"A mezuzah was stolen from Isabel's house Friday night. Did she show you where it was hidden?"

"Yes."

"Whoever took it may have been the person who ran me off the road."

"Possible," Romero said.

"It couldn't have been Tony," Claire said.

"No, but it could have been one of his homeboys."

"How would a homeboy know where to look and what would he want with a mezuzah?" she asked. "It's not likely to have any monetary value."

"It might," Romero said. "Anything has value if it's old enough, and according to Tey it was very old. The other things stolen from the house didn't have much value."

"Except for the last words of Joaquín Rodriguez."

"We don't know yet if that document *was* stolen or what its value is," Romero pointed out. "We haven't found any evidence that it was offered for sale."

The image of him in casual clothes faded as he took the official line. Today Detective Romero seemed very much a police officer. Perhaps he was putting on his armor for his next call. "Did you find any evidence that the dig had been disturbed?" she asked.

"The OMI archaeologists looked into it. Someone had

sifted through the dirt, but we don't know who. Family members were in the house. It could have been one of them.

Tey agreed to have her DNA analyzed and compared to the skeleton."

"So she said."

"We're setting it up with the OMI and they will work with the Smithsonian. That man died four hundred years ago. It will be interesting to know if he is a Santos but I don't see how it will help solve Isabel's death. It's unlikely anyone killed her just for being a Marrano."

"May Brennan had reason to think the Santoses were crypto Jews. A couple of years ago she asked Tey about her background."

"It would be hard to get my boss to consider May a suspect, if that's what you're suggesting. She's been in Bernalillo for a long time. She's the town historian."

As a middle-aged white professional woman she didn't fit the criminal profile. It was the same profile Claire benefited or suffered from, depending on her point of view at the time. She'd thought before that the profile was a good façade to hide behind. In fact, it almost gave one license to commit a crime.

"For me it goes back to the document," she said. "I believe someone wanted Joaquín Rodriguez's last words. Isabel got in the way and got killed. The mezuzah in Isabel's house proved that the Santoses had a Jewish connection and the killer didn't want that fact known. I read Peter Beck's book last night. He described Joaquín Rodriguez's execution. Joaquín had a conversation with a man in the crowd who held a green cross, maybe even the same cross we found in the house. I'm wondering if that man ended up with Joaquín's last words and brought them to New Mexico. Beck published an article about the identity of the man, but I haven't been able to locate a copy."

She'd been hoping to pique Romero's interest in the historical aspects but sensed failure as he shifted his weight from one side of the chair to the other.

"It's interesting," he said, "but it doesn't compare to having a gangbanger in custody who tried to fence Isabel's VCR."

"Have you found any record of Isabel depositing money or calling anyone who might be a suspect?"

"No deposits and the only people she called were you and family members."

"You could examine *their* records."

"They'd have to be suspects first."

"What about May Brennan? Have you examined her bank account or phone records?" Claire's despair over Isabel's death was greater than her guilt about implicating May.

"She'd have to be a suspect, too," Romero said. "What you've come across is real interesting for a historian and an academic, but I don't think Lieutenant Kearns will see it as motive for homicide." He moved to the edge of his chair. "Anything else? I need to get going."

"That's it," Claire said.

She walked him out to the exit and said good-bye. He hadn't seemed totally unsympathetic, just busy, preoccupied about his boss like anybody else with a job. She was glad her own boss was at a meeting, and she didn't have to worry about him seeing her with a policeman. On her way down the hall she glanced at the wall clock. Four. She couldn't stand another minute in her hermetically sealed office. It was either open the door and the blinds, let the world in, or leave. She picked up her keys and her purse and left.

chapter twenty-five

On her way home she stopped at Page One, Too to see John Harlan. He wasn't a historian, but his work took him into the past. When she told him about her conversation with Tey Santos, he ran his hand over the top of his head, making his hair stand up like it had been electrified.

"You're lucky to find someone who would talk to you about that subject. It's not information they reveal to just anybody."

"I don't know if I'm lucky or unlucky. I think the Santoses' background has something to do with Isabel's death, but it's hard to get the police to see it that way."

"A gangster in the hand is worth a lot of speculation in the bush," said John.

"She also told me the Jews were known as the people of the book."

"Just like you and me," John said.

Claire sat down, cleared a space on John's messy desk and rested her arm there. "I read Peter Beck's book on the Inquisition last night."

"Is that why you look so tired?"

Do I look that bad? she wondered. "Not exactly. Beck's description said Joaquín Rodriguez was led through the streets to the burning ground with a green cross tied between his hands. He encountered a young man also carrying a cross. Something about that encounter convinced the Inquisitor Manuel Santos that Joaquín had converted and it saved him from being burned alive. I did a computer search for more information and discovered that Peter Beck published an article in the *Historical Journal of the Americas* titled "The Identity of the Man in the Crowd at the Inquisition of Joaquín Rodriguez.""

"But you couldn't find the article?"

"I put out an interlibrary loan request but haven't gotten the article back yet. Sometimes it takes awhile."

"And you want me to help?" John had the ability to spot a customer from across the room. He turned his nose up like he'd caught the scent of a rare and sought-after document.

"Right."

"Is it ephemera?"

"That would depend on how you define ephemera."

"I define it as printed material that doesn't have a spine thick enough to display writing."

"Then I would say that it is. As I remember the *Historical Journal of the Americas* didn't have a spine."

"Do you care if I ask Warren Isles? If the article has anything to do with New Mexico he may have picked it up somewhere. That journal occasionally published articles about our state, which would be enough for someone as obsessive as Warren to collect every issue."

Warren Isles gave Claire the same uneasy feeling as Peter Beck. She didn't trust either one of them. "I'd rather you didn't. Warren will connect you to me and if he has anything to hide, I don't want him to make that connection."

"Warren has a devious mind, but I can see right through him. If he has anything to hide, I'd know it."

"It would be better if you didn't contact him."

"Okay. I suppose you've got some reason for not asking Peter Beck himself."

"I don't trust him either."

"He teaches at Berkeley, right?"

"Right."

"Combine Berserkeley with academentia and what do you get?"

Claire's brain was too tired to wrap itself around that crazy thought. "You tell me."

"Double jeopardy, double insanity."

And what would that produce, Claire wondered, a paranoid schizophrenic? Alzheimer's could be considered a form of insanity, too, she supposed, as the mind slipped further and further from its moorings.

"What are you doing for dinner?" John asked.

Claire hadn't gotten to dinner yet. She was so tired all she had thought about was going home and going to bed. "I'm hoping I'll find something delicious in my freezer."

"You want to stop at Emilio's? It's on your way home."

"I'm so tired."

"Have a glass of wine. It'll revive you for a little while."

"Okay," Claire agreed.

She waited for John to finish his business, then they walked across the parking lot to their vehicles.

As she reached for the door of her rental car, John said, "Wait a minute. Where did that come from?"

"Did I forget to tell you that my truck was in a wreck?" Claire asked, wondering what else exhaustion had caused her to forget.

"How'd that happen?"

"Someone ran me off the ditch road on Friday night. I had just passed Isabel Santos's house on my way to Tey's. I wasn't hurt, but my truck was wrecked."

"That's what's wrong with you. You're suffering from Chevy deprivation."

"Maybe," Claire said.

"See you at Emilio's."

Claire had two glasses of wine at dinner and laughed at all of John's jokes. After dinner he walked her to her car, hesitated, poked the pavement with the toe of his shoe, then said, "Listen, I can follow you home if you want."

"I only had two glasses of wine," Claire said. "I'm sober."

"That's not what I'm worrying about. I don't want someone to try to run you off Tramway."

"I'll be all right," Claire said.

"You sure?"

"Yeah. Someone may have cared about my going by Isabel Santos's house, but I don't think anyone cares what I do on Tramway."

She got home safe, parked the rental car in the garage, and let herself into the house. Ignoring Nemesis's pleas for attention, she went right to bed and fell into a deep sleep.

After a decent night's sleep, Celia's bracelets made a pleasant tinkling sound. Or was she wearing fewer of them? Claire wondered when her friend appeared in her office.

"I haven't found Peter Beck's article yet," she said.

"I'm not surprised. I doubt it had a very wide distribution."

"But I talked to my friend at Berkeley. She told me that Richard Joslin's wife, Renee, cares for him at home in Oakland. The brilliant, independent scholar has become a helpless, absent-minded professor. Can you imagine what it must be like to care for a husband with Alzheimer's? When the mind goes, so goes the heart. Love is based on memory and shared moments. How can it continue without memory? Richard still has moments of lucidity, my friend said. I got his number if you want to call."

"What good would it do to call a man with Alzheimer's?"

"I'm sure Renee answers the phone. She worked in the department, too, and may remember the Peter Beck incident. My friend told me that Joslin was Beck's mentor so I'm sure it hurt to be rebuked by him."

She handed Claire a piece of paper with the number on it. "Go for it," she said.

Claire couldn't convince herself to make the call while she was at work, but when she got home she wrote down all the reasons she should, skipped all the reasons she shouldn't, prepared what she would say to Renee Joslin and dialed the number. She heard the phone being removed from the hook but no one spoke.

"Hello?" she said into the void.

"Hello?" a man's voice echoed.

"I have a question for Richard Joslin. Is he there?"

"Is Richard Joslin here? Yes." The man answered his own question. "He's here. Would you like to speak to him?"

He seemed borderline lucid. Not knowing how long the moment would last, she spoke fast, trying to keep her question simple but not so simple as to imply he was dumb. "My name is Claire Reynier. I'm a librarian at the Center for Southwest Research at the University of New Mexico. I'm doing some research on the Jewish mystic Joaquín Rodriguez and I'm looking for an article Peter Beck wrote about the identity of a man at his Inquisition. The article was supplemental reading for one of your courses." First she'd see if he remembered the article, then she'd ask why he disagreed with it.

"Peter Beck," was all he said.

She had no idea what to say next. Not wanting to challenge him she resorted to "he's a brilliant scholar."

"Peter Beck," he said again with a deep sadness in his voice. For the Peter Beck he remembered or the Peter Beck he did not? He paused and Claire had an image of him trying to pull facts out of an empty hat. "The father and the son," he said. If the father was the first fact, Claire thought as she waited for Richard Joslin to continue, the son would be the second. Joslin seemed to catch his breath and then his voice turned stubborn and angry. "Not so brilliant. He said the Jew became the son. But there's no proof. Sloppy scholarship. Pure speculation."

"Richard," Claire heard a woman say in the tired voice of a scold. "What are you doing? Whom are you talking to?"

"I don't know," Richard replied.

It was tempting for Claire to pretend she was an automated call and hang up, but that seemed dishonorable.

"Hello?" the woman's voice said into the phone.

"Is this Mrs. Joslin?"

"Yes?" the woman said, changing her tone to the annoyed voice reserved for credit card solicitors.

Claire suspected that if she said she was calling on behalf of Visa or MasterCard Renee Joslin would hang up and that would be the end of it, but she took a chance and identified herself. "My name is Claire Reynier. I'm a librarian at the University of New Mexico."

"Oh?"

"I'm doing research into the Mexican Inquisition and I'm looking for an article written by Peter Beck," she said although she feared her query might make its way back to Peter Beck.

"Did you ask my husband about *that*?"

"Yes."

"You've upset him. Please don't call here ever again."

Claire's ear rang as Renee banged down the phone. Alzheimer's wasn't a physically contagious illness, but the mental frustration it caused spread like ink seeping into a blotter. She went outside, listened to the cicadas strumming in the trees and watched night fall behind the West Mesa. The lights in the Rio Grande Valley twinkled on. The sky near the horizon was the blue-green twilight color that follows a sunset. A bright light appeared in the west that might have been an approaching plane but hovered in place long enough for Claire to determine it was the planet Venus. She had read that Venus was always visible in the sky and people could train themselves to see it even in the daytime.

As she watched the other planets and stars come out, pieces of the Rodriguez/Santos puzzle began to fall into place. "The father and the son," could be Richard Joslin and Peter

Beck. She didn't know whether Joslin had his own son, but the mentor might have thought of the student as a son. "The Jew became the son." She sent that phrase into the night and waited to see what came back.

She saw a sprinkling of what-ifs that mirrored the lights on the ground and the stars in the sky. What if the Catholic family that adopted the orphan Daniel Rodriguez happened to be the family of Manuel Santos, the Inquisitor? It had to have been a family with good standing in the church. What if Daniel became Manuel's adopted son and took his name? What if he was the young man who approached Joaquín Rodriguez on his way to the *quemadero* then persuaded Manuel Santos to give his brother a less painful death? What if Daniel Rodriguez was the ancestor of the current Santos family and he was the one buried with Joaquín's last words under the house on Calle Luna?

What if this was the information contained in Peter Beck's article and he lied when he said he believed Joaquín Rodriguez's conversion was sincere? After his book came out, he might have come across long-hidden records in the archives in Mexico City stating that Daniel Rodriguez was given to Manuel Santos to raise. But there might have been no written evidence that Daniel Rodriguez took Manuel Santos's name and found his way to New Mexico until Joaquín's last words showed up inside a cross with specks of green paint.

For Peter Beck it would be the solution to an intellectual puzzle, proof of his hypothesis. He'd be unlikely to feel any emotional connection to the people involved. But for Claire, thinking that Daniel Rodriguez had made his way to New Mexico and brought his brother's last words with him, that the beliefs of Joaquín were honored by Tey Santos 400 years later, was a discovery as magical as the night sky. She wanted to gift wrap the discovery, put a bow on it and deliver it to Tey, but first she needed to be sure and that meant finding Peter's article.

She looked up again before she went inside. The sky was black velvet and thousands of stars were visible. They all seemed to be in place, but stars and planets had no fixed place in the sky. Their location changed with the days and the seasons. Tomorrow Venus wouldn't be exactly where it was today and next month it would be somewhere else.

She went inside and called May Brennan again. After she heard May's recorded voice mail message she said "May, this is Claire. I need to talk to you. Please call me back." It was getting close to ten o'clock. She believed May was home and screening her calls. She couldn't make May answer her phone so she gave up and went to bed.

chapter twenty-six

It would take time to track down Peter's article. The response from interlibrary loan had not been encouraging; several copies of the journal were reported missing. Waiting was frustrating but Claire trusted the people who were searching on her behalf—August, Harold, John, and Celia. She didn't want to be a nudge and bother them every day so she kept quiet and waited. On Thursday Mauricio Casados, the mechanic in Bernalillo, called to say her truck was ready.

"Yay!" she said.

She returned her rental car after work and got a ride to Bernalillo with a coworker who lived in Placitas.

The mechanic's hands were covered with grease. His smile was missing a tooth. But to Claire he was beautiful.

"Good as new," he said, handing over the keys.

The truck looked almost new, better than it had before the wreck. Mauricio had taken out all the small old dings along with all the large new ones, but vehicles that were in major accidents often didn't achieve the alignment they had before. Her expression had to show doubt because Mauricio asked if she would like to take the truck for a ride to make sure it was all right.

She agreed and took it for a drive around Bernalillo before she paid him.

"Rides good, no?" he asked.

"Yes," she agreed.

On her drive she saw that Silva's Saloon on Camino del Pueblo was having one of its occasional poetry readings. After she paid Mauricio she stopped in. Silva's walls were a collage of photographs and magazine clippings featuring decades of women, dogs, and motorcycles. The poet reading in the back room was a Lakota Sioux from South Dakota. Claire sat on a stool at the bar, ordered a glass of white wine and listened to him read. He had an easy style and a subtle sense of humor. He was followed by another poet in a pair of dirty overalls who looked like a Jemez hippie. Next came an Albuquerque poet who wore an elegant pair of hand tooled cowboy boots but whose poetry lacked finesse. She paid for her drink, asked for directions to May Brennan's house and left.

It was nearly eight o'clock. May was sure to be home from work by now. Although she had known May for years, Claire had never been to her house. Considering her interest in history she expected to find a restored adobe, but May lived in a frame stucco ranch, bland enough for suburbia, but lacking a suburban lawn. Her yard had a few sad weeds and some thorny Russian thistle that would turn into tumbleweed and move on at the end of summer. The car parked in the driveway was a Subaru Outback. Beneath layers of dust it was black, but too small to be the vehicle that ran Claire off the road unless her imagination had blown that event way out of proportion.

She parked in front of the house, straightened her back, walked up the path to the front door and pushed the bell. She saw TV light flickering behind a lace curtain.

"Coming," May called. She yanked the door open and said, "Oh . . ."

Expectation segued into disappointment in her distracted eyes. Claire wondered just who May had been expecting.

"What are you doing in Bernalillo?" she asked.

"I was having some work done on my truck. I came to pick it up."

"You came all the way to Bernalillo to have work done on your truck?"

"It was in a wreck here. If you'd answered my calls, I would have told you about it."

"I've been busy," May said.

She didn't look like she'd been busy. She looked like she barely had the energy to get off the sofa. May's divorce had aged her. Her spine had compressed from lack of calcium or lack of energy. It brought her hips and breasts too close together and gave her the rounded shape of a muffin.

"Can I come in?" Claire asked.

May's expression protested, "Do you have to?" but her words were a lackadaisical "Sure, why not?"

She led the way into the living room decorated in baby blue recliners with foot rests that popped up when the sitter leaned back, the kind of furniture Claire swore she would never put in her own house no matter how long she lived. May picked a stack of newspapers off the sofa and cleared a spot for Claire. She returned to her armchair, leaned back and the footrest snapped into place with military precision. She picked the remote off the coffee table and dropped it in her lap but didn't bother to turn off the television set or even to lower the volume. She didn't offer Claire anything to drink. The house felt damp and had a musty smell as if she had been running her swamp cooler 24/7.

A woman with a normal sense of curiosity would have asked Claire about her wreck. May kept silent so Claire answered her own question. "I was on my way to Tey Santos's house by way of the ditch road last Friday and someone ran me off the road into a cottonwood."

May lifted herself out of her lethargy long enough to inquire, "Were you hurt?"

"Not really, but there was a lot of damage to my truck. Mauricio Casados fixed it."

"He's a good mechanic. Why were you going to Tey's house?"

"To talk to her about Isabel's death."

"I hear she believes Tony Atencio is responsible." May's voice had more hope in it than belief.

"Not any more. Something else was stolen from the house Friday. Tony Atencio is still in jail." Claire moved to the edge of the sofa. "Do you know anything about Isabel Santos you're not telling me?"

"No, of course not. Why do you think that?"

"Because of the way you've been acting. You've never tried to avoid me before."

"I said I've been busy."

"So busy that you're willing to let a murderer get away?"

May sat up. The foot rest fell forward and collapsed beneath the chair. "What's your problem, Claire? As far as I know Tony Atencio was responsible. Why are you bugging me about it? This has been a hard time and now Rex has a girlfriend. Look at this." May picked up a newspaper clipping lying on the end table and handed it to Claire. "She's young, she's beautiful, she's skinny. She's everything I'm not."

It was a photograph of Rex and another woman arm in arm at a charity event. Rex looked paunchier and balder than Claire remembered. The woman *was* thinner than May, but in Claire's eyes she wasn't beautiful and she wasn't all that young. She had the skinny, undeveloped body of an adolescent, but her thinness emphasized the wrinkles in her face. Her hair was blonde and bouffant and she wore a lot of Indian jewelry. It made Claire think that sooner or later you have to grow up and develop a woman's style, but that didn't have to mean getting sloppy and matronly like May. She wouldn't tell May that, but she thought some firmness was in order.

"I know how much it hurts, May, but you've got to move on and make a new life. You're letting your breakup with Rex interfere with your work and obscure your judgment."

"Easy enough for you to say," May snapped.

"It's not easy for me to say, but I know you can't sit around wallowing in self-pity."

"At least you were able to get out of town."

"It helped. It sounds trite, I know, but fixing yourself up, losing weight, getting your hair done, taking a trip, buying new clothes—all those things will make you feel better."

"I'll never be glamorous no matter how many spas I go to or how much money I spend."

"Maybe not, but you're smart, you're interesting. You have a job you love. You're respected in this town. Keep putting one foot in front of the other, doing your best day by day. Get out of your recliner. You'll get through this. You'll get your self-respect back." Claire balanced on the edge of the sofa and lowered her voice to a conspiratorial whisper. "Tell me what you know about Isabel's death, May. It's important."

May sighed and leaned into her recliner. Claire was afraid the chair would tip back, the foot rest would pop up and May would sink further into her depression. Since they seemed to have fallen into some kind of push/pull dynamic, she slid back into the sofa and spoke in a conciliatory voice. "It can't be that bad, can it?"

"I don't know how bad it is, Claire. I told some people about the document Isabel found. Maybe I shouldn't have."

"Why not?"

"She asked me not to."

"Then why did you tell people?

"Honestly? I did it because I wanted to impress them. In our world, finding the last words of Joaquín Rodriguez will get you more respect than being young and beautiful."

"You knew those were his last words?"

"Who else would say 'the fire or the garrote'? The way she described the document I knew it was authentic, too." Her eyes burned with the fire of discovery as she turned into the May Claire used to know.

"But you never actually saw it?"

"No. I wanted to put it in the Historical Society safe, but Isabel wouldn't let me. She said she was going to take it home and decide what to do. I gave her your name first and then Peter Beck's and Warren Isles's. After she left, I called them and her brother Manuel. Isabel was known to have problems with drugs. I was afraid she might sell it for drug money. I thought Manuel should know."

"How did those men react when you told them?"
"Peter and Warren got greedy. They wanted to see it. Manuel asked me what it meant and what it was worth. I said I didn't know exactly what it was worth, but I knew it was valuable."

"Did you give him Peter and Warren's names, too?"

"Yes, and I regretted it considering what happened."

"Why didn't you tell the police?"

"I felt guilty. Then I felt scared. Thoughts that used to be field mice when I was married have become grizzly bears now that I live alone. The police had a good suspect. They seemed to think Tony Atencio was guilty. Why not leave it at that?"

"Was Manuel curious about how the words of a Jew ended up under the floor of his family's house?"

"Somewhat. Manuel's a politician and a lawyer. He keeps his cards close to his vest."

"Are people in this town afraid of him?"

"I think they're more proud than afraid. The people in Bernalillo identify with him and want him to succeed."

"I've been looking for an article Peter Beck published in the *Historical Journal of the Americas*. Would the Historical Society have a copy?"

"We might if it had to do with New Mexico history, although Peter Beck's scholarship tends to stop at the border."

"It has to do with the Inquisition of Joaquín Rodriguez, but it might reveal how his last words got to Bernalillo."

"I'll look for it tomorrow. It would be thrilling if the skeleton under the floor turns out to be Manuel Santos, the settler."

"How would he have gotten hold of Joaquín Rodriguez's last words?" Claire had her own theory now, but she was interested in May's opinion.

"He was related to Manuel Santos, the Inquisitor, and that Manuel Santos wanted those words to be far away from Mexico City. He wouldn't want it known that he had been unable to convert Joaquín."

"Why not just destroy the document?"

"The Spanish were too compulsive to destroy documents."

"Have you ever heard of a crypto Jew taking the name of an Inquisitor?"

"They were known to take the names of prominent citizens. An Inquisitor would seem like the last name a Jew would want, but it would provide good cover. No one in New Mexico would reveal that fact to me, even if they knew. The crypto Jews have been covering up for so long, they don't even know their own truth. If I don't find Peter's article, I could ask him for a copy."

"I'd rather you didn't."

May didn't question Claire's reticence and she was grateful she didn't have to explain. Maybe she was working on the same intuitive level as Claire. Maybe she didn't trust Peter either. Claire gave May a hug when she left, feeling that if she had accomplished nothing else on this visit she'd at least pulled her out of the depths of her recliner.

In the morning May called to say she couldn't find the *Historical Journal of the Americas* that contained Peter Beck's article. Claire broke her own rule and called John Harlan and August Stevenson.

"Hey," John said. "I've been lookin' for that ephemera, but I can't find the damn thing anywhere. Every time I feel like I'm gettin' close it seems like somebody gets there just ahead of me. You want me to keep trying?"

"Please." After she hung up she called August.

"I've been searching, Claire," he said in his slow as a tortoise voice. "But I haven't found it. I ran into Warren Isles at the Palace Restaurant the other day and I mentioned I was interested. He said he'd let me know if he came across one."

"Did you tell him you were looking for me?"

"No, of course not. I told him I'd been working for UC Berkeley."

Claire wondered how hard it would be to link August's inquiry to her. Since they were in the same line of work, it was reasonable for Warren to assume they knew each other.

chapter twenty-seven

 When she got to her office on Monday morning Claire found a message on her voice mail, apparently left by Warren Isles on Sunday night.

"Ms. Reynier," he said. "I have a document that will interest you. I'll be at Tamaya tomorrow and can meet you there at six-thirty. If you are available please leave a message for me at the front desk."

Claire called his brokerage office in Santa Fe and learned that Mr. Isles would be out all day. She tried his home number and got a recorded message. Since she was unable to connect with the man who preferred to meet face to face, she played his message several times listening for nuance and innuendo. He had said "document" and not "article." He'd said you "will" be interested in rather than "may" or "might." Was it possible that he had Joaquín's last words or was that just wishful thinking on her part? It was like him to control the time and place of the meeting and to choose Tamaya as the setting. She hated to be manipulated, but she needed to see what he had. She called Tamaya and left a message at the front desk saying she would meet him at six-thirty.

She spent the rest of the day calculating what time she should leave and whether she should bring her own check book or the one she used to buy collectibles for the center. It took forty minutes to get to Tamaya. She could leave at five-forty, arrive in plenty of time and be left cooling her heels in the lobby or on the deck. Both were beautiful places to wait, but how long would she have to wait? How long had she and John waited the last time? A half hour? Some chronically late people were so predictable, you could almost set your watch by them which would seem to defeat their purpose. Could she count on Warren Isles to be half an hour late again? The master manipulators were unpredictable. Sometimes it was half an hour, sometimes an hour, sometimes they didn't show up at all, occasionally they even arrived on time. If Warren's goal was to keep her off balance and persuade her to pay too much for whatever document he produced, he'd keep her waiting a long time, so long that she would end up feeling angry and defeated while he'd be elated by the power he had over her. She hated to be kept waiting, and he may have observed that on their previous meeting. The benefit of arriving late on her part was that she might be less angry when he finally showed. He might actually end up waiting for her. If she had any spine, she thought, she would leave at six and arrive at six-forty, but she was as compulsively on time as Warren Isles was late. When it got down to it, she wasn't capable of even leaving at five forty-five. At five-thirty she got in her truck and drove to Tamaya.

She made excellent time and arrived at six-ten. She parked in the first space she came to on the south side of the building away from the main entrance. Since she had time to kill, she refused a ride in the jitney cruising the lot and walked. The sun was low enough in the sky now for her to cast a long legged shadow, but it still had the searing, burning heat that gave mystics their vision, the heat in which nothing mattered but truth or shelter.

She still had a few minutes left when she entered the hotel, and spent them in the shop looking at the Southwestern clothing and jewelry—the broomstick pleated skirts, the patterned vests and jackets, the elaborate concha belts that no one from Albuquerque would buy and wear. She considered them costumes rather than clothing.

It was a small victory to arrive at the front desk at exactly six-thirty, better at least than getting there early. The desk clerk was busy checking someone in so she walked across the lobby to look at the David Michael Kennedy photos of Indian ceremonial dancers. They were beautifully framed and had the soft edges of old photographs. Her favorite was the hoop dancer. His foot was lifted, his arms extended, one hoop was raised to the sky and the other lowered toward the ground. The dancer seemed trapped in suspension somewhere between anticipation and animation.

"May I help you?" the clerk asked in a courteous, respectful manner.

Claire returned to the desk. "I have an appointment with Warren Isles."

He checked his computer. "Mr. Isles left a message that he has been unavoidably detained. He will be here at eight."

"Thank you," Claire said, making an effort to be as polite as the clerk. She turned and walked across the lobby, glancing at the hoop dancer again. She had the illusion that he'd moved his foot a fraction while she'd looked away.

She went into the living room and sat on a sofa facing a fireplace with an Edward Curtis print above the mantle. She'd seen that particular print numerous times and felt no need to study it again. She stared at the fake logs in the fireplace. Tamaya burned gas here, not wood, better for the environment, but lacking the crackle, heat and wildness of a wood fire always in danger of getting out of control. She wished she could strike a match and start a real fire instead of seething within. It might be considered thoughtful of Warren Isles to leave her a message instead of letting her wait and wait and wait. Now she knew how long she had to wait if he showed up at eight, but he might not. At eight there might be another message saying he'd be later or wasn't coming or there would be no message at all and she'd be put on hold again. What was he doing? Showing his document to someone else and trying to get a better price? Eating dinner? Having a massage? Playing golf? Stuck in nonexistent traffic somewhere between Tamaya and Santa Fe?

She got up and went into the bar wondering if she might see Warren or anyone else she knew. She didn't. She could have one of Tamaya's oversized Margaritas, which would either calm her down or make her angrier. For some people provoking anger was a sign of power, which, to them, had to be better than not getting any reaction at all. As a person Warren was lacking in looks, talent, charm and intellect. It was the things he owned that gave him his power. Since she wanted something he owned, she had to find a productive way to pass the time.

She decided to walk in the Bosque where the wandering branches of the cottonwoods offered cool, green shelter. She thought about taking her purse back to her truck, but it was a long walk from here. Tamaya was a place that would look after its guests. As she crossed the field the trees shimmered like a green mirage. The temperature dropped ten degrees once she stepped under the branches. She followed the trail that curved and wandered through the woods seeing no one else. Eventually the path led to the open banks of the Rio Grande where the cottonwoods had been destroyed by flood or by fire. New trees had been planted but they were still small and the banks of the river were bare except for the occasional red twigs of salt cedar. The river was shallow here but the current ran strong. From above the water was a muddy brown, but from an angle it was even bluer than the sky. A flock of small, dark, unidentifiable birds cawed and flew over. Claire sat down on a solitary bench beside the river, stared at the Sandias and waited for the sun to set off an afterglow. It seemed to hover just before dropping behind the horizon as if preparing to release its power. A hawk flew in and circled lazily over the river causing the flock of small birds to squawk and scatter. As it turned in its gyre, the sun caught its white underbelly and burnished it gold.

The only sound Claire could hear was the lapping of the river. In the silence and the beauty, she tried to put human greed aside and focus on the golden hawk. A branch snapped behind her. She turned and saw nothing but the shadows in the woods. She glanced at her watch. Seven-twenty. She could head back now or wait until the sunset ended. She waited, watching the rosy afterglow climb the mountains as the western sky turned orange. The sun dropped behind the horizon, the glow lifted off the peaks, the hawk flew north. A vulture dropped into a tree. A coyote on the east side of the river began to yip. She got up and headed back to the hotel without checking her watch, thinking the best way to deal with Warren Isles was not to focus on time. The meeting would happen when it was supposed to happen or it wouldn't.

Shadows filled the Bosque. The leaves rustled in a breeze that picked up as soon as the sun went down. The gravel path crunched beneath her feet. The coyote began a lonesome howl. Claire was glad she'd encountered no one at the river, but in the growing darkness she would like to have seen a runner or a friendly face. She did what she usually did when threatened by darkness and isolation, took her key ring from her purse and inserted the keys between her fingers. Up ahead she saw lights in the crotches of the cottonwoods and beyond that the yellow lights of Tamaya. She walked faster, drawn like a moth to the artificial light. As she neared the edge of the Bosque, the tree lights illuminated the curving branches and the shifting shapes of the leaves. The path opened to a panoramic view of the hotel, which resembled a spacious country home hosting a private party. People sat in the lights on the deck laughing and drinking, giving Claire the feeling that they were golden, privileged, and much further away from her than the width of the field.

A branch snapped in the woods. As she swiveled sideways to see, she heard the crunch of gravel behind her. She turned in that direction and saw a swirling shadow or a person hiding under the hood of a cape.

"What do you want?" she cried.

The figure raised its arm holding something in its hand. A bat? A branch? She watched it with a strange sense of detachment. This can't be happening to me, Claire Reynier, a voice inside her brain said. Then the weapon came down hard on the place where her shoulder met her neck. The blow knocked her to the ground. As she fell, her purse was yanked from her arm and her keys dropped out of her fingers. She saw the golden glow of Tamaya flickering through the trees and then it went out.

chapter twenty-eight

She came to in the dirt with a branch beside her head and the feeling she'd been dragged into a place with oversized trees toppled upside down and illuminated by lights. From where she lay the twisting shapes looked more like roots than branches. She had no idea how long she had been out. She tried lifting her head from the ground and felt a sharp pain in her shoulder and a dull pain in her head. She rolled over onto her stomach, hoping to get to her knees and raise herself from that position. She heard distant laughter, saw the lights from the deck and thought there must be a party somewhere. Then she remembered she had come to Tamaya to talk to Warren Isles. Someone had attacked her on the gravel path, but there was no gravel beneath her now, just soft dirt created by millenniums of floods. She got to her knees. The pain in her right shoulder was intense. She pushed with her left hand and sat up. There was enough light from the trees to see that her purse was not in the dirt beside her.

Was it possible someone had attacked her just to steal her purse? She tried to remember what she had heard or seen of the thief, but all she could recall was the sense of a shadow in motion. What had happened to her keys? They'd been useless for defense, but she needed them to get into her truck. She crawled along the ground using her left arm and her knees like a three-legged animal, heading for the direction where the path should be, stopping periodically to run her hand across the dirt and feel for the keys. It was slow and uncomfortable going not knowing whether her assailant would return. She heard footsteps crunching the gravel up ahead, the sound of someone running. She saw the shape of the runner just beyond the trees. She thought of calling to him but feared he could be her assailant.

At least she'd learned where the path was. She crawled to it, feeling for her keys, making her way around fallen twigs and branches. The path became visible with scuff marks in the gravel from boots and shoes. She remembered she'd fallen near the edge of the woods and headed in that direction. Crawling on the path made her too visible and the gravel scraped her hand and knees so she crawled beside it in the dirt. She came to a spot where the gravel had been brushed aside, reminding her of the sliding marks of children making angels in the snow. This was where she'd fallen, but she hadn't really fallen. She'd been surprised and knocked down just like Isabel Santos had been. This attack may have had more to do with Isabel Santos than with anything in her purse.

She felt around the edges of the scuff marks, reaching onto the path and into the woods until her hand landed on the jagged edges of her keys. "Yes," she whispered. She picked them up, crawled back into the woods and considered what to do next. There was a tiny flashlight at the edge of her key chain but she hesitated to use it and call attention to herself. She had to ignore the part of her that wanted to curl up in a ball and hide here like a wounded animal. She could scream for help, but that might attract the wrong person. She needed to get to the cell phone in her car and call Jimmy Romero; she trusted him more than anybody inside Tamaya.

She pressed her back against the rough bark of a cottonwood and worked her way up until she reached a standing position. Getting there was painful but once she was standing she reached a sort of equilibrium. She straightened her spine and neck, and her shoulder and head didn't hurt so much. She took a step forward. Her head spun and she leaned back against the tree. When her head cleared she took a second step and then another. There were plenty of trees to lean on when she got dizzy. With this thought in mind she worked her way through the Bosque along the edge of the field stepping from one tree to the next, aiming for the parking lot and the shelter of her truck.

Ahead of her something flapped in the wind. A solid shadow took shape among the sinuous Bosque branches. Had her assailant returned in the cape? She pressed herself against a tree. The shadow moved, caught a breeze, became a bad memory. Claire tried to blend into her cottonwood. The wind lifted the edge of the shadow and beneath it she saw the limbs of a tree, not the limbs of a person. Someone had disposed of the cape by tossing it over a branch. She went to the branch, picked up the cape and found her purse lying on the ground beneath it. She took the cape and the purse with her, planning to wait until she was inside her truck before examining them.

Where had her assailant gone? she wondered. Back to the hotel, to a vehicle in the parking lot, or was that person still in the woods? She remembered the cavalier coyote trotting across the field totally oblivious to its audience. Her neck hurt but she felt less woozy now, less in need of a tree to lean on. She had to cross the field to get to her truck and she stepped into the open space. She was outside the circle of the light and the people on the deck were within it. They couldn't see her but she could see them. She was close enough that if she screamed they might hear. In the field she could see if anyone was coming.

She walked across the open space, glad now that she had parked at this end of the lot. She approached with her keys between her fingers, since the shape of a vehicle could be concealing her assailant. The keys hadn't worked earlier, but it was the only protection she had. When she reached her truck, she inserted the keys in the lock, pulled the handle and let herself in. She didn't want to call attention to herself by turning on the overhead light. Using the light on the end of her key chain, she looked through her purse. Her checkbook was there and so was her wallet. Her credit cards and driver's license were all in place. Only the $50 she'd been carrying in cash was missing. Had cash been the motive or had the thief been looking for something else?

Claire took an aspirin from her purse and washed it down with the bottled water she kept in the truck. She beamed the light over her clothes then on the reflection of her face in the rear view mirror. Her forehead was scratched and bruised. There was dirt on her hands and knees, twigs and leaves in her hair, the alarm of the hunted in her eyes. She couldn't go inside Tamaya looking like prey.

Her watch said it was close to nine, an hour more or less since she'd been attacked. How much of that time had she been unconscious? Long enough for her assailant to drag her off the path and into the woods. Long enough to cause a rupture in the artery of awareness. She wondered what the thief had done during the past hour? Driven away, gone deeper into the woods, returned to Tamaya?

She picked up her cell phone and held it in her hand, knowing she should call Detective Romero but not wanting to reveal she'd been attacked once again with no proof. She didn't want to be seen as a person who couldn't get out of harm's way, or even worse as a woman capable of imagining she was in harm's way. She wanted to give Romero something other than shadows to go on. A description of the assailant or the assailant's vehicle would help. A license plate number would be even better. It was possible the assailant's vehicle was still in the lot. No one would have walked all the way to Tamaya to attack her.

She started her truck, turned on the headlights, stepped on the gas and drove at a snail's pace to the end of her row in the parking lot. The leg on the gas pedal had a tremor. Her shoulder hurt when she turned her head. Negotiating a parking lot could be almost as difficult as driving in heavy traffic. You never knew when another driver would do something unpredictable or back out of a space without warning. The rows were narrow and dangerous. But Claire drove so slowly if anything happened it would be a bump and not a crash. She saw safety in the number of vehicles in the lot. Most were empty but any one might contain a witness.

When she reached the end of her row, Claire turned and drove down the next one, then she turned again making a series of hairpin turns while she searched the lot. Her eyes were drawn to black SUVs. There were almost as many here as there were white rental cars at the airport, too many for any one to stand out. They came in many brands: Izuzu, GMC, Chevy, Ford, Subaru, Honda, BMW. She saw New Mexico plates, Colorado plates, Arizona plates, Texas plates,

California plates. She saw no way to identify the SUV that had run her off the road if it was even here.

She was ready to give up and dial Detective Romero's number when she thought she saw someone she recognized step out of the jitney transporting guests from the hotel to their vehicles. It was a row away so it was hard to be sure. The person clicked a remote and turned on the lights of a vehicle, but it wasn't a black SUV. It was a medium-sized white car similar to the one Claire had rented. The driver got into it and began to back out of the parking space.

Not wishing to be seen Claire turned off her lights. The car headed for the exit road. She pulled out, too. When the car turned left at the road, she followed. As soon as she turned onto the narrow road she flipped on her high beams making it harder for the other driver to see and identify her truck. She forgot about the tremor in her leg and the pain in her shoulder as she negotiated the road that was barely wider than her Chevy. Her thoughts were on getting the license plate number and how fast she could go without spinning off the road into the desert. When she reached the 17 miles per hour sign she was doing 25 and not getting any closer to the car. When she picked up speed, it did, too, making it difficult to narrow the gap between them and get close enough to read the plate. Claire slowed down and let the gap grow, hoping the car might go slower if the driver didn't feel pursued, hoping to catch up at the stop sign.

By the 27 miles per hour sign she was three or four car lengths behind. She negotiated the last curve and stepped on the gas planning to read the plate when the car stopped. But the other driver ignored the stop sign, swinging wide and turning onto the two-lane road. Holding her breath, Claire clutched the steering wheel and swung wide, too. One wheel teetered on the place where the desert met the road but she held tight and straightened out again. The white car picked up speed—50, 55, 60. This road was wider and straighter than the other one. Claire could go faster here but not this fast. She looked down at her speedometer—65 and not gaining an inch. Feeling connected to this car by a tether, she tried slowing down again, lifting her foot from the pedal, falling behind, remembering that there was a traffic light ahead at Route 44 that was impossible to ignore.

For the first time ever she was pleased to see a red light. The white car had stopped and there was no one between them. She was almost close enough to read the numbers when the light turned green. The car sped through and turned left onto 44. Claire followed. Cars were feeding into Route 44 from 528 and the traffic became her ally. She blended into the flow and closed in on the white car, which could only go as fast as the traffic allowed. When she thought she was close enough to read the plate, she swung into the white car's lane, got behind it and read the critical numbers. She repeated them out loud a few times and then over and over silently until they were etched in her brain. She dropped back and let other vehicles fill the space between her and the white car. There was no need to be bumper to bumper now, only to be close enough to see where the car turned off.

She watched it head south at I-25, then she turned onto the road that led to the cemetery, parked and dialed Detective Romero's cell phone number.

"This is Claire Reynier," she said when he answered the call.

"Hey. Are you all right?"

She relayed what had happened and gave him the license plate number. It was a relief to get it out of her mind and into his. "The car turned south on I-25," she said. "It looked like a rental car. It could be headed for the airport."

"We'll stop it and question the driver. Wait for me there."

"I'm too exposed here," Claire said. "Do you have permission to operate on the Santa Ana Pueblo?"

"Yeah. They're too small to have their own force."

"Then I'll meet you at Tamaya." Claire hung up before Romero tried to change her mind.

chapter twenty-nine

When she got back to the hotel she parked as close to the door as she could and accepted the ride offered by the jitney driver. The well-dressed couple on board looked at her with the distaste reserved for bag ladies and rodents. Her trump card for respectability had always been that she was a middle-aged woman but it wasn't working with them. They were middle-aged, too, and infinitely more respectable right now than she was. The couple squeezed into the corner, getting as far away from her as possible. The driver passed the bronze fountain and parked in front of Tamaya's entrance. A fire burned in the outdoor fireplace. Claire wanted to stand in front of it and absorb its warmth, but she went to the shop instead.

The clerk gave her a wary welcome. Guests might come here after a round of golf but not after crawling through the Bosque. Golf wasn't a contact sport.

Claire improvised. "I was in a minor car accident," she said. "I'm meeting someone for dinner and I can't show up looking like this. Could I buy some clothes, wash up and change?" Her purse dangled from her shoulder. She took it off and rested it on the counter in front of the clerk. The only card she held now was Visa.

"Okay," the clerk replied.

Claire picked some dresses off the rack, tried them on and bought the first one that fit. It was denim with a broomstick pleated skirt, silver buttons on the bodice and Lots of Santa Fe Style, more of a disguise than a dress. She thought this might be a good time to step out of character.

"That's an improvement," the clerk said as she rang up the sale.

The dress was too expensive but Claire paid the price, went to the ladies room, washed up, massaged her sore shoulder, dressed, combed her hair and put on some makeup. She put her own dress in the bag the store provided and walked out to the lobby to wait for Detective Romero. She was surprised to see him already there, standing by the entrance wearing the Sheriff's Department uniform that made him hard to ignore.

"Ms. Reynier?" he asked.

"You got here fast," she replied.

"I was in Placitas when I got your call. You look different. I almost didn't recognize you."

"I was a mess. I had to buy some new clothes." Just in case he had any doubts she opened the bag to show him the dirty dress she'd been wearing when she was attacked.

"Warren Isles is registered," Romero said. "He took a room for the night, but he's not there. I need your help to find him. I don't know what the guy looks like."

"He looks plump and prosperous," Claire said.

"Everybody here looks like that."

"Let's try the bar," Claire suggested.

As they walked through the living room and into the bar,

the hotel guests pulled back when they saw a police uniform. Romero didn't seem to notice, but Claire did. She supposed he'd gotten used to being treated like an unwelcome intruder. Fires burned in the fireplaces on the deck. People sat in the light drinking and laughing. They were the golden, privileged people who seemed so remote when Claire was in the Bosque. Now that she'd joined them they appeared more human.

Warren Isles wasn't in the bar and she didn't see anyone else she knew.

"Let's try the restaurants," she said.

They walked down the stairs to the medium-priced restaurant, which was framed by layers of stone that reminded Claire of the ruins of Chaco Canyon.

"This is a beautiful place," Romero said.

There weren't many diners left at this hour. They circled the room but didn't see Warren Isles. They went outside and followed the path to Corn Maiden, the more expensive restaurant, which was still half-full. Did people who paid more eat later or linger longer? Claire wondered.

She picked out Warren as soon as they stepped into the restaurant. He sat alone at his table in a chair that faced the door. There was no one left at the adjacent tables. The ceiling light was overhead. His skin had a ruddy tone as if he'd played golf that afternoon or taken a sauna. His hair seemed slick, maybe even damp. It was possible he'd attacked her, taken a shower, dressed and come here for dinner. He'd had time. When he saw her approach he looked at his watch.

"That's him," Claire said.

There was a sleek attaché case at Warren's feet, an expensive and nearly empty bottle of wine on the table, a clean plate. He had a full and self-satisfied glow. He smiled his half-moon smile as they approached.

"Claire," he said. "Didn't we have an appointment for six-thirty?"

"I was here at six-thirty," Claire replied, "and was told you were unavailable and would meet me at eight."

"Really? I didn't leave that message. I was in the lobby then waiting for you. Nice dress. The color becomes you. I'm Warren Isles," he said.

"Detective Romero," the detective replied.

"Have a seat. Please." He waved his hand at the empty chairs around the table. "The salmon is superb. I recommend it."

Claire wanted to sit down but Detective Romero remained standing, hovering over the table, and she followed his lead.

"I brought a document here that I thought would interest you," Warren said to Claire. "I heard talk in Santa Fe that you were looking for a *Historical Journal of the Americas.*"

Her proximity to the food, the wine and Peter's article made Claire feel weak and famished. "May I see it?"

Warren flipped his half moon smile into a fake frown. "I don't have the journal any more. You didn't show up and I had another customer."

Warren Isles would never come to Tamaya to see one customer if two would get him a better price. Romero stood still, letting Claire and Warren dance this dance. She was grateful to him for that.

"I received such a good offer that I had no choice but to part with it. After all, it was only a scholarly article with a limited market."

"Who made the offer?"

"Peter Beck. The author of the article."

Claire longed to sit down now but remained standing

trying not to show anger, weak knees or any other feeling while Detective Romero took charge.

"When exactly did this transaction take place?" he asked.

"Forty-five minutes ago more or less," Warren said. "I asked him to join me for dinner but he was in a rush."

"And where is this Peter Beck now?" Romero asked.

"Catching a late flight back to California I suspect."

"He came all the way from California to buy this journal from you?"

"He wanted it very badly. It's an article he wrote several years ago. I gather he had very few copies left."

Romero stared at the attaché case beside Warren's foot. "Do you always bring your briefcase to dinner?"

"Only when I'm conducting business."

"Do you care to show me what else is in it?"

The emotions played across Warren's face as he calculated what was good for Warren and what was best for Warren.

"Do you have a warrant?" he asked.

"No, but someone attacked Ms. Reynier in the Bosque while she was waiting for you. I could bring you in for questioning and hold you until I get a warrant."

"You were attacked?" Warren asked. "I'm shocked. No damage was done, I hope. You look well."

"I changed my clothes and cleaned up," Claire said.

Warren took a deep sip of his wine. "I had no idea you were attacked. I didn't even know you were here. Of course I will show you what is in my briefcase." He picked it up, placed it on the table, keyed in the combination and snapped open the brass latch.

A small document encased in plastic lay on top of a pile of papers. The paper inside the document was crinkled and had rough edges. The words written in ink in an elegant script were faded but legible. They had survived for more than 400 years in New Mexico's dry climate. To Claire it was a voice from the grave. She leaned close and read "*Todo sta de arriva abasho. El fuego o el garrote. Dame el fuego. Adonay es me dio. Joaquín.*"

The tremor in her knee got out of control and she had to sit down. "Where did this come from?" she asked.

"Peter Beck. In exchange for his article and a considerable amount of my money, he gave it to me. Here." Warren Isles slid his plump fingers inside the protective cover and touched the precious paper that held Joaquín Rodriguez's last words.

"Leave it alone," Romero said, while Claire thought of the wine, the butter, the salmon Warren had eaten for dinner, the greasy fingerprints he was putting on a priceless document.

Warren removed his fingers.

"You are aware, aren't you, that this is evidence in a murder investigation?" Romero asked.

"Lieutenant Kearns told me that when he interviewed me. I intended to bring it to the Sheriff's Department just as soon as I finished dinner."

"How did Peter Beck explain having the document in his possession?" Romero asked.

"He says Isabel sold it to him. He claims he had nothing to do with her death and that she was fine when he saw her last. He feared the document would be lost or damaged if he turned it over to the police as evidence."

"Did you read his article before you sold it to him?" Claire asked.

"Yes. In fact I made a Xerox copy. You might find it useful.

Do you mind?" he asked Romero as he reached for the case again.

"Are there any other valuable documents in there?" Detective Romero asked Warren while he looked at Claire.

She couldn't think of anything. Besides, everything in the briefcase already had Warren's fingerprints on it.

"Just the usual ephemera," Warren said. He flipped through the papers until he found the one he was looking for and handed it to Claire.

He and Romero parried while Claire read the Xerox of the article, learning, just as she had expected, that an archivist in Mexico City presented Peter with long lost documentation that the orphan Daniel Rodriguez was given to Manuel Santos to raise, that he took his adopted father's name, that he left Mexico City and came north with Oñate's expedition in 1598. It was Peter's theory that Daniel stepped out of the crowd and spoke to his brother as he was led to the burning ground. That Daniel convinced the Inquisitor Manuel Santos not to burn his brother alive. Peter admitted it was quite possible there had been no conversion, which would mean the words now in Detective Romero's possession represented Joaquín Rodriguez's last feelings.

This was the theory the scholar and mentor Richard Joslin questioned. It remained unproven until the cross and the document turned up under Isabel Santos' floor and tied the Santos family to the Rodriguezes. Peter Beck was the one person who knew exactly what Isabel's find meant. Had Isabel refused to sell it to him? Claire wondered. Had Peter Beck lost his temper and killed her accidentally or with intent? He'd ended up with the document that proved his theory, but what good had it done him? It resembled having a stolen Van Gogh in the closet, a guilty pleasure to admire but impossible to share with anyone else; to do so would implicate him in Isabel's death. Claire had seen Beck drive away in the white car. He could well have been the one who attacked her in the Bosque wrapped in the black cape and armed with the viciousness of an Inquisitor. But what about the person who ran her off the road and stole the mezuzah from Isabel's house? The mezuzah was evidence that the Santoses had a crypto Jewish connection. Peter might wish to have it in his possession and hide that evidence, but where was the black SUV?

Warren Isles was also a skillful liar, and they only had his word for how the document ended up in his briefcase.

"Have you and Peter ever met before?" she asked Warren.

"As a matter of fact, we met the same day I first met you. I was curious about the document. He wasn't willing to admit he had it at that point, but he did ask me to find copies of his article."

"What kind of a car do you drive?" Romero asked.

"A Jaguar. It's in the parking lot. Would you like to see it?"

"Yes," Romero said. His cell phone rang. He listened for a few minutes then said, "We're in the Corn Maiden Restaurant."

"Backup has arrived," he said to Claire. "And Peter Beck was apprehended on I-25." He turned to Warren. "He claims that you were in possession of Joaquín Rodriguez's last words and tried to sell them to him."

"Well, that's a lie. When you examine the document I'm sure you will find Peter's fingerprints all over it."

And he'd covered himself by putting his own fingerprints on it, thought Claire. What else would the physical evidence show? Anything Peter or Warren said could be dismissed as self-serving.

"We're bringing both of you in for questioning," Detective Romero said.

"You're arresting me here in the Corn Maiden?" Warren asked.

"Only if you don't come in voluntarily."

"Well then, of course, I'd be happy to help," Warren said.

chapter thirty

Romero's backup was the deputies Claire had met earlier—Anna Ortiz and Michael Daniels. Deputy Ortiz was assigned to take Claire's statement. Romero and Daniels took Warren out to the parking lot to examine his Jaguar and then to the detention facility.

By now the last few diners had left the Corn Maiden. Only the staff remained, and they were busy shutting down for the night. Claire opened her purse to demonstrate to Deputy Ortiz that nothing but cash had been taken.

"I need to take your purse and wallet to test for prints," Ortiz said, "but you can keep your credit cards, driver's license and ID. Show me where you were attacked. I'll take your statement there."

"All right," Claire said, although she had no desire to return to the Bosque.

Anna Ortiz's Sheriff's Department vehicle earned her a parking space right in front of the hotel entrance. They drove to Claire's truck.

Claire handed her the black cape which became a hooded poncho once the lights were turned on.

"The assailant wore this when he attacked you?" Ortiz asked.

"Yes. I found it later in the woods with my purse."

"We'll check it for evidence."

The emblem on Ortiz's car also gave her permission to drive across the field and they were back at the Bosque all too soon. They found the spot where Claire had been knocked down. To her the dirt looked like it had been disturbed by wings. They walked through the woods to the tree where she had found the poncho and her purse. The Bosque that had seemed so gray and spooky earlier, became black and white under the beam of Ortiz's flashlight.

They returned to the car where Ortiz called for someone to guard the crime scene. Then she took Claire's statement.

Once the statement was finished and more deputies had arrived, she drove Claire to her truck. "Are you all right to drive home?" she asked. "Can I follow you?"

"I'll be all right." Claire felt better as time went by.

"Take care," Deputy Ortiz said. "We'll be in touch."

Claire took the interstate back to Albuquerque wondering if she might see a white car beside the road or any sign of Peter Beck's arrest. She didn't. Lightning flashed, splitting open the darkness above the West Mesa. When she got home she gave Nemesis his dinner, worked the stiffness out of her shoulder with a shower massage, took a painkiller and climbed into bed.

Hours later the sound of thunder woke her. The clap was so loud and close she expected the smell of ozone to fill her house. She calculated lightning had struck ground somewhere in the nearby Sandias. The reverberating sound of thunder brought back the pain in her shoulder and the fear of the day. Next came the sound of rain, a rushing, purging, cleansing rain that turned the drainage arroyos to white water rapids. Any animals on the prowl would be scurrying for cover. As she lay awake listening, Claire remembered she'd been in the middle of a dream when the thunder clapped. She'd been chasing a white rabbit down a narrow, winding road. The rabbit came to a hole and hopped in. She followed, tumbling through emptiness until she landed in a hall of mirrors with gigantic images of the duplicitous faces of Peter Beck and Warren Isles facing each other. Whatever statements they gave were smoke and mirrors. In this case physical evidence was everything.

The thunder clapped again, but it didn't shake her house this time. It sounded as if it had moved to the far side of the Sandias, a sign the storm was heading east. The rush of the rain was over. Now it had the gentle, pinging sounds of the strings of a guitar. It soothed her pain and lulled her to sleep.

When the pain woke her in the morning, she took some aspirin and went to work. Later in the day Romero called and confirmed that Peter Beck's and Warren Isles's statements were self-serving and contradictory. Each claimed the other had tried to sell him the document. Both of their prints were on it. They released Warren but were holding Peter until his house in California could be searched. A *Historical Journal of the Americas* was found in his car along with considerable cash, far more cash than Warren Isles carried. Claire was convinced Peter had attacked her, but she would have felt safer if Warren had been incarcerated, too.

"Have you released Tony Atencio?" she asked.

"Not yet."

When they got off the phone she called Harold Marcus and told him the Sheriff's Department was holding Peter Beck in custody as a suspect in the death of Isabel Santos.

"You think he killed her over the document?" Harold asked. "There's a man who takes his work far too seriously."

"He found evidence in the archives in Mexico City that Manuel Santos adopted Daniel Rodriguez, Joaquín's brother, and that Daniel took Manuel Santos's name. It would be wonderful if we could prove that Daniel brought his brother's last words with him to Bernalillo."

"The staff here is working on the DNA analysis and testing the tooth enamel. We should have the results soon," Harold said.

"Thanks," Claire replied.

It was a long week. Every morning Celia poked her head into Claire's office and asked, "Heard anything yet?"

And every morning Claire had to answer, "No."

Romero called on Friday to ask if he could stop by her office.

"Of course," Claire said.

"What time would be good for you?"

"After three," she said. That was when Harrison left for the weekend.

"I'll be there," Romero said. He didn't bother to stop at the Information Desk this time and surprised Claire by knocking on her office door a few minutes after three.

He sat down in the visitor's chair and said, "We released Tony Atencio on bail. He'll be tried for theft, but Beck's our suspect in Isabel's death. He's a college professor. Atencio's a gangbanger. But you know there really isn't a lot of difference between 'em. They're both the kind of guys who will do anything to make their names come out and feel important. Atencio didn't lie to us, anyway. Beck did."

Claire saw disappointment in his face that the academic world he had admired at a distance turned out to be no better than the petty criminal world he dealt with every day. She didn't know his world, but she'd lost any illusions she had about academia once she took her first job at the U of A.

"We established that Beck flew to Albuquerque four times this summer," Romero continued. "Once on the day Isabel Santos died, once to talk to us, once on the day you met Warren at Tamaya and were attacked at the Santos house and once more on the day we arrested him. On every trip he used a different airline and rental car company. Hertz rented him the SUV. Did he think he was concealing his actions by spreading his business around? The guy may be a brilliant scholar, but some of his other actions weren't too smart."

"Scholars are better at work than they are at life," Claire said. "People who can write a brilliant book can't fix a leaking faucet."

"Beck likes silk shirts," Romero said. "The fiber we found, which was on Isabel's clothes, matched a shirt in his closet. We never did make a fiber match with Tony Atencio. We located the SUV Beck rented, took paint samples and matched the paint found on your bumper. Tey Santos identified the mezuzah that was in Beck's safe deposit box. He must have gone back to the house looking for anything that could tie him to Isabel's death."

"The mezuzah proves that the Santos family had a Jewish connection and Peter Beck was probably the only person outside the family who knew that."

"We also found twenty copies of the *Journal* with his article in it. Some of them were library copies. It would have been better for him if he had destroyed the stuff."

"Historians are packrats," Claire said. "It's impossible for them to destroy anything."

Romero's eyes circled the crowded bookshelves in her office, and Claire wondered if he thought she was a packrat, too.

"The article proves Beck knew the Santoses were descended from Daniel Rodriguez. He must have known that a smart person like you . . ." Romero smiled at Claire.

She smiled back.

" . . .would track the article down and come to the conclusion that once Beck heard a document from the Inquisition was found in the house of a family named Santos, he would want it badly."

"It proved his hypothesis. My thought was that once I had the article in hand I could persuade you to investigate Beck further, to get a warrant and search his house."

"When we confronted him with the evidence we had, he admitted he'd been to Isabel's but he claimed she was alive when he left. He says Isabel sold the document to him, but there is no record he took any money out of his accounts to pay her. We believe Isabel refused to sell. There was an argument that became a physical struggle. Isabel fell on top of her purse with the cross inside, or else Beck would have grabbed that, too. He panicked, took the document and left the house. In our opinion Isabel was dead at that point. If he'd left her alive, she would have been able to ID him."

"I suppose he justified taking the document by convincing himself that something could have happened to it if he left it there."

"Something might have. Tony Atencio or even Manuel Santos could have destroyed it. But if Beck had called us, we would have taken care of the document. If Isabel was still alive, we would have taken care of her."

"But then Peter would have had to admit what he'd done."

"Better to have admitted it right away. The longer he denies it, the tougher the prosecutor's gonna be. If he'd come clean immediately, we wouldn't have any more crimes to charge him with. What do you think? Was he trying to kill you or just stop you from connecting with Warren?" Romero moved forward in his chair and Claire saw curiosity and concern in his eyes.

"I don't know," she answered. It wasn't a subject she enjoyed thinking about. "Runners use the trail. Peter was in plain sight and he didn't have much time. A murder in the Bosque would have been investigated a lot more thoroughly than a mugging. A murder investigation might have led to Peter. I also think he's a coward who runs away when he's in trouble. By selling the document to Warren, he preserved it. Possession would have made Warren a suspect in Isabel's death if you hadn't accumulated all the other evidence."

"Most of the evidence we have is circumstantial, but we have a lot of it. It's just a question of what he'll be charged with."

"Did anyone else in the family receive money from him?" Claire asked.

"There's no evidence of that."

"Who paid off Chuy's gambling debts?"

"Manuel. It was bad for his image to have a brother way deep in debt. We couldn't get any prints from the poncho or your purse, but we traced a call from Beck's cell phone to the front desk at Tamaya around the time the message was left that Warren would be late. There's no evidence Warren ever made that call himself. Beck will be arraigned on Monday morning. I thought you might like to be there."

"I would."

Romero stood up. "We've set up a meeting with the family after the arraignment to talk about the document and the mezuzah. The OMI says they should have the results of the DNA comparison by then. Can you come?"

"Yes," Claire said. She stood up, too.

"See you at the meeting," Romero said.

He knew the way so Claire didn't walk him out to the exit. She stood in her doorway and watched until he turned the corner.

chapter thirty-one

She arrived early for the arraignment, took a seat and watched the courthouse fill up. Chuy, wearing clean jeans and a T-shirt, escorted his grandmother down the aisle. Tey's hand resembled the talons of a hawk as she gripped his arm. Manuel was smooth and handsome in a dark suit. He brought his blonde wife who also wore an expensive suit. They sat apart from Tey and Chuy. Lieutenant Kearns and Detective Romero were present, too.

Peter Beck had only been in custody a short time, but Claire saw a pronounced change in his appearance. He wore a prison uniform. He was pale. His gray pony tail was limp and pencil thin. He had hired a prominent lawyer from Albuquerque.

The prosecutor, Joe Burgess, was a stocky, athletic-looking man who clapped his hands for emphasis. He seemed confident. And why wouldn't he be? Claire thought. Premeditation and first degree murder would be difficult to prove, but he was only charging Peter Beck with grand larceny, assault and battery and murder in the second degree.

When asked how he wished to plead, Peter replied "not

guilty" to all the charges. Claire didn't hear confidence in his voice. She heard contempt for the charge, for the process, for the court that tried him. He didn't sound like he ever intended to plea bargain, but she thought he might be better off if he did. The case against him seemed solid. She was sure he would do time, but not as much as he deserved.

Before he left the courtroom, Peter raised his head high which made his nose seem even more prominent. He turned and scanned the crowd. It would be his last look at his accusers before the trial began. He acted like he wanted to fix them in his brain, take the image back to his cell, examine it and probe for weaknesses. He skipped over Manuel, lingered on Tey and Chuy. Then his gray eyes landed on Claire. He took a deep breath and his nostrils widened. His lips turned into a sneer. She saw no remorse in his expression, only anger that he had been caught. She felt that if she were a student and this were a lecture hall, he would eviscerate her with words, humiliate her and cut her work to ribbons before the class. She hoped Peter Beck would never lecture again. She hoped he would stay in prison for the rest of his life and if there were any further victims of his anger, they would be fellow inmates.

When the arraignment was over, the family, the investigators, and Claire met in Joe Burgess's office. Lieutenant Kearns thanked Claire for her help. If he had any doubts about her involvement he seemed to have pushed them far back in his mind.

Claire sat down beside Tey and took her hand. "I know you're glad this is all over."

"It won't be over until that dude is locked up for good," Chuy said.

"Almost over," Claire corrected herself.

"Thank you very much," Tey said, squeezing Claire's

hand, "for helping us find my Isabelita's killer. When I saw that man's eyes I knew he was the one. That man does not deserve to be a teacher."

"He deserves to be a prisoner," Chuy said.

Manuel Santos came alone to the meeting. He thanked Claire and shook her hand, but his eyes never met hers. She felt he wished she had had nothing to do with this. He would have preferred that Tony Atencio had been charged with the crime and he didn't have to deal with the weight of his family's past, that he would rather be known as Manuel Santos the Catholic than Manuel Santos the crypto Jew whose sister was killed over an historic family document. It was a conflict known to split families in two.

When everyone else was seated, Lieutenant Kearns stood, opened the file he held and said, "I have received the report on the skeleton from the Office of the Medical Investigator. I know you're all very interested to hear what it says. The Smithsonian and OMI couldn't establish for sure if he is Daniel Rodriguez or Manuel Santos, whatever name you want to use, but there is a DNA match to Tey. He is definitely your ancestor."

"*A la*," Chuy said.

Manuel looked out the window and said nothing.

"By strontium testing of the tooth enamel the Smithsonian established that your ancestor spent his youth in Portugal in the late sixteenth century," Kearns said.

"Does that coincide with what you know about the Rodriguez family history?" Joe Burgess asked Claire.

"Yes. According to Peter Beck's book, Daniel Rodriguez spent his childhood in Portugal before the family emigrated to Mexico. Peter's scholarship in the book has never been questioned."

"I'd like to have a copy," Burgess said. "Can you get me one?"

"Yes."

"Would you be willing to testify as an expert at the trial?" Burgess asked.

"I'd be glad to help, but I'm not an expert, just an interested party. I can refer you to some experts." May Brennan came to mind.

"I'll get in touch with you later about it," Joe Burgess said. He clapped his hands and Kearns picked up the beat.

"The cross was also dated to the late sixteenth century," Kearns said. "I'm the first to admit that I don't know much about history, but it looks like the skeleton is Daniel Rodriguez and he brought his brother's last words to Bernalillo with him hidden inside the cross."

"It's obvious those are Joaquín Rodriguez's words, but it's impossible to establish they were his last words," Manuel, the lawyer said, already beginning his defense of the family's Catholicism. "Joaquín's conversion to Catholicism could have been sincere, and Daniel could have converted to Catholicism, too."

It was possible, but Claire didn't believe it. Tey had too many connections to Judaism. She knew that Catholicism and Judaism were issues that would never be resolved in some families. As the centuries went by and the number of descendents increased, some became devout Catholics, some remained fervent Jews, some were neither. When it came to religious beliefs, there was no proof.

"A mezuzah is a box with a Hebrew prayer inside, right?" Joe Burgess asked anyone willing to provide an answer.

"It's a prayer to keep the house safe," Tey said.

Lieutenant Kearns showed them the mezuzah tucked inside an evidence bag.

"This is the one we found in Peter Beck's safe deposit box. We need to keep it as evidence, but we should be able to give it back to you after the trial is over," Joe Burgess said.

Then Lieutenant Kearns displayed Joaquín's faded and elegant last words also in an evidence bag. Claire caught her breath; the document was so significant, so old, so valuable. It was incredible it had endured for four hundred years and could still speak.

"Isabel showed this document to you, is that correct?" Joe Burgess asked Manuel.

"Yes," he admitted.

It was the first Claire had heard of this. She reviewed her conversation with Manuel at the duck pond, wishing she had recorded it on tape. As she recalled he implied there had never been a document, but had he actually said so? She suspected if she replayed the conversation she'd find it was all innuendo, that Manuel was too careful a lawyer to lie to her.

"It's the document she showed me, but I knew nothing about Joaquín then. I asked her not to say anything until I could find out more, but May Brennan called Peter Beck and he went to the house. I thought when Tony Atencio robbed the house the document got destroyed in the robbery."

Not telling anyone this earlier bordered on criminal activity in Claire's mind but she supposed that prosecuting Manuel Santos for concealing the truth wouldn't help the case against Peter Beck.

"We will need to keep this until the trial is over, too," Lieutenant Kearns said, displaying the cross, also in an evidence bag. It was the cross Isabel had protected when she fell. All together the cross, the mezuzah, and the document were potent symbols of the family's complicated past and present.

"As a family, you need to start thinking about what to do with these objects when you get them back," Burgess said. "My only suggestion is that you put them in a very safe place."

"We will do that," Tey said.

"We'll be talking to all of you again before we go to trial. Does anyone have any questions for now?" the prosecutor asked.

No one did.

"Okay then." He gave one final clap. "We're done here."

Detective Romero had sat in the back of the room and kept quiet during this meeting. Lieutenant Kearns hadn't taken all the credit for solving the crime, but he hadn't given any to Romero either. Claire caught up to him at the door and walked him down the hall.

"I hope you get credit for the work you did," she said. "Your open-mindedness and your availability made it possible to catch Peter Beck. If it weren't for you, Tony Atencio would still be in jail."

"Thanks," Romero said. "You did a pretty good job yourself."

They stood in the hallway, smiling and congratulating each other until Tey came along and tapped Claire on the arm. "Chuy and I are going to visit Isabelita's grave now," she said. "Can you come with us?"

"Yes," Claire said.

"We will meet you there."

Claire took her time as she walked out to her car in the parking lot. One remaining question she had was the kind of vehicle Manuel Santos drove. She knew it wasn't the SUV that ran her off the road, but she wanted to know if Chuy had been telling her the truth when he told her it was gray. She was relieved to see him step into a gray SUV and drive away. It was one less lie to ponder.

When Claire got to the cemetery, Chuy was helping his grandmother step down from his truck. She heard the traffic whiz by on the Interstate and the sign at the trailer lot flap in the breeze. They walked to Isabel's grave at Tey's leisurely pace. It took discipline to slow down and walk as slowly as Tey did, but once Claire made the transition she felt the benefits. She no longer heard or saw the Interstate. She had time to focus on what was close up, time to remember and look back at the past. Getting the cemetery to reveal its secrets was like turning the pages of a book. She saw the red cloth flowers on Isabel's grave. Claire knew now they hadn't been put there by Tey. They stood in front of the tombstone for a few minutes while Chuy remembered the past.

"Isabel, Manuel, and I saw that mezuzah in the closet when we were little," he said. "We wondered what it was, but it seemed like a secret of the house so we put it back. We saw you lighting the candles and blowing the smoke around, Grandma. We remembered you and our father and uncles chanting in a language we didn't understand. Sometimes we wondered if we were Marranos. That was before Manuel became so Catholic."

"Did you tell your father this?" Tey asked.

"No. It was like it was your secret."

"I wish I had told Isabelita before she died. It's something the women pass on." Tey touched the tombstone. "My precious, why didn't you come to me when you found that paper?"

"I'm sure Manuel told her not to," Chuy said. "He didn't want anybody else to know."

"That's the way the Catholics are," Tey said. "They only know one truth. It's too bad we have to bury our people here with them. I'm telling you this now, Chuy, because who knows if I will be alive when we get that paper back. I want you to give it to Claire. I want UNM to keep it. I don't care who knows about us now."

"Okay, Grandma," Chuy said.

"We'll take good care of it," Claire said. "I promise."

"I know you will. Now I want you to show me what you discovered at the other Isabel Santos grave."

They walked across the graveyard keeping to Tey's measured beat. They passed the graves of the soldiers who died in Vietnam, Korea, World War II and World War I, the children who died too young, and the couples who were *juntos para siempre*. They passed the section where the nuns were buried and approached the place where the jackrabbit lived and the gravesites were marked by wooden crosses lying on the ground. At the edge of this section they found the grave of Isabel and Moises Suazo.

Claire pointed out the six petalled flower. "It could be interpreted as the symbol of the Star of David," she said. "And the faint carving of a candelabra—that could be a menorah. I sketched the flower and the symbol in the middle and I faxed it to Harold Marcus at the Smithsonian. It could be a stamen in the flower but he interpreted it as a shin. That's the twenty-second letter of the Hebrew alphabet and the first letter of shema, the prayer Jews say." Claire hoped she was getting the essence of what Harold told her if not the literal meaning. "It means 'Hear O Israel, the Lord is our God, the Lord is One.'"

"*Adonay es mi dio*," Tey said. "He is with me when I walk along the way. I love him with all my heart." She'd been holding a pebble in her hand and she placed it on Isabel Santos de Suazo's tombstone.

The sound the stone made resonated. Claire thought of the millions of years it took to turn sand and water into stone, how ancient the Hebrew prayers were, how timeless Adonay.

They walked slowly back to Isabel's grave. Tey picked up another pebble and placed it on top of her tombstone.

"*Descance en paz, mi nieta*," she said.

Claire heard the flapping sound. It was only the breeze lifting and dropping the edge of a sign, but to her it had the echo of the beating wings of time.

OTHER JUDITH VAN GIESON BOOKS IN THE
CLAIRE REYNIER MYSTERY SERIES

Vanishing Point
ISBN 0-8263-2383-9

The Stolen Blue
ISBN 0-8263-2233-6

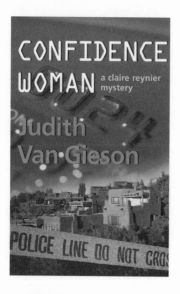

Confidence Woman
ISBN 0-8263-2888-1

University of **New Mexico** Press

1-800-249-7737

www.unmpress.com

OTHER JUDITH VAN GIESON BOOKS IN THE
NEIL HAMEL MYSTERY SERIES

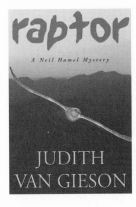

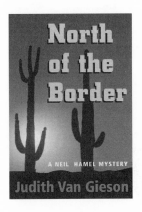

Raptor
ISBN 0-8263-2974-8

North of the Border
ISBN 0-8263-2886-5

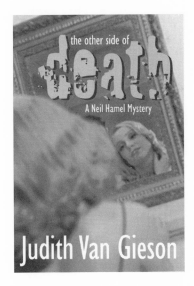

The Other Side of Death
ISBN 0-8263-3207-2

 University of **New Mexico** Press
1-800-249-7737
www.unmpress.com